CARLA CASSIDY

Special Agent's Surrender

ROMANTIC
SUSPENSE

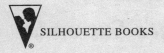

SILHOUETTE BOOKS

PLEASE RECYCLE
THIS PRODUCT IS RECYCLABLE

Recycling programs
for this product may
not exist in your area.

ISBN-13: 978-0-373-27718-6

SPECIAL AGENT'S SURRENDER

Copyright © 2011 by Carla Bracale

This edition published by arrangement with Harlequin Books S.A.

For questions and comments about the quality of this book please contact us at Customer_eCare@Harlequin.ca.

® and TM are trademarks of Harlequin Books S.A., used under license. Trademarks indicated with ® are registered in the United States Patent and Trademark Office, the Canadian Trade Marks Office and in other countries.

Visit Silhouette Books at www.eHarlequin.com

Printed in U.S.A.

Books by Carla Cassidy

Silhouette Romantic Suspense

*The Delaney Heirs
**Cherokee Corners
‡ Wild West Bodyguards
‡‡Lawmen of Black Rock

CARLA CASSIDY

is an award-winning author who has written more than fifty books for Silhouette Books. In 1995, she won Best Silhouette Romance from *RT Book Reviews* for *Anything for Danny*. In 1998, she also won a Career Achievement Award for Best Innovative Series from *RT Book Reviews*.

Carla believes the only thing better than curling up with a good book to read is sitting down at the computer with a good story to write. She's looking forward to writing many more books and bringing hours of pleasure to readers.

Dear Reader,

Yes, it's true. We're changing our name! After over twenty-five years of being part of Harlequin Enterprises, Silhouette Books will officially seal the merger by taking the company's name.

So if you notice a few changes on the covers starting April 2011—Silhouette Special Edition becoming Harlequin Special Edition, Silhouette Desire becoming Harlequin Desire and Silhouette Romantic Suspense becoming Harlequin Romantic Suspense—don't be concerned.

We'll continue to have the same fantastic authors, wonderful stories, eye-catching covers and emotional, compelling reads. We're just going to be moving under the overall company name, which will make us even easier for you to see in the stores, on the internet, and wherever you usually find us!

So look for the new logo, but remember, beneath the image will be the same promise of romantic stories of love, passion, adventure, family and a whole lot more. Just the way you like them!

Sincerely,

The Editors at Harlequin Books

Chapter 1

It had been another long, quiet day at the real estate office. In the current economy nobody was buying or selling property in the small town of Black Rock, Kansas.

Layla West shuffled her feet beneath her desk, seeking her newest pair of navy sling-back heels. If there was one thing in the world that Layla loved it was shoes. There was also the fact that she'd been left with an inheritance that allowed her to remain calm despite the fact she hadn't made a sale in a month.

With high heels in place, she rose from the desk and grabbed her coffee mug. As she carried it into the back room where there was a bathroom, she noted that darkness had fallen outside.

At least it hadn't snowed yet, she thought as she dumped the last of the tepid coffee down the sink. Early-December often brought winter weather to the small prairie town.

Coffee mug rinsed, she returned to the front office and grabbed her coat from the back of her chair. It was time to get home to her cat, Mr. Whiskers, the only male who seemed content to stick around with her for the long run.

With her coat around her shoulders and her purse in her hand, she locked up the office and stepped outside. She looked around to make sure nobody was lurking nearby and then headed down the street where her car was parked against the curb.

She'd stayed late in hopes that somebody might call, and because she'd been reluctant to go home where lately the silence, the loneliness, had begun to press in around her.

The streets were deserted, most of the stores having closed not long before. She picked up her pace, uncomfortable with being out alone after dark.

She noticed that the streetlight above where she'd parked had burned out and made a mental note to mention it to Sheriff Tom Grayson. The candy cane decorations hanging from all the streetlights reminded her that it was time to get her little fake Christmas tree out of its box and go wild with all her other seasonal decorations. She loved Christmas and always went nuts decorating her house.

Eager to get inside and get the heat blowing, she started to open the car door and realized she'd left her cell phone on her desk in the office.

"Nobody is going to call you," she muttered aloud. Besides, she had a landline at home if anyone really wanted to get in touch with her.

Deciding to get the cell phone in the morning when she returned to work, she quickly unlocked the car, slid in and punched her key into the ignition.

Before she could turn the key an arm snaked around the back of the seat and against her neck. A scream tried to escape her as the arm applied pressure to her throat.

For a moment she thought it was some kind of a weird joke, an old boyfriend trying to scare her, a friend playing a prank, but that momentary thought fled as the pressure on her throat increased, cutting off her airflow.

Wildly, she glanced at the rearview mirror, but realized it had been flipped up so she couldn't see who was in her backseat, who was trying to choke her.

Her first instinct was to grab at the arm, to scratch and claw in an effort to get free. A searing fear gutted her as she thrashed against the seat. Her head pressed against the headrest as the arm tightened; her attacker did not make a sound as he squeezed the air from her lungs.

This isn't a joke, her mind screamed as her vision was narrowed by encroaching darkness. The candy cane decoration hanging from the nearest streetlight began to blur and fade as first tears, then stars danced in front of her eyes.

She tried to scream again, but it came out only as a strangled sob. He was going to kill her. He was going to choke the life out of her. Tears once again blurred her vision and she knew if she didn't do something quickly she was going to die.

The arm around her throat was strong and she knew she didn't have the strength to pull it away and would waste precious energy in the effort. As she realized she couldn't break his hold, she did the only other thing she could think of—she pulled her foot up and took off one of her high heels. Using the heel as a weapon she slammed it back over her head.

There was a low grunt and the pressure against her neck momentarily eased. As she drew in a rasping gasp of breath she slammed her hands down on the car horn.

As it blared in the otherwise silent streets, the attacker jumped out of the car and raced off into the darkness of the night.

She hit her automatic door locks and began to cry in deep, gulping sobs. Still she held down the horn, a bleating plea for help as she squeezed her eyes tightly closed.

Dear God, what had just happened? Why had it happened and who had it been? The questions couldn't maintain any weight as terror still fired through her.

She'd almost been killed. She forcefully coughed, as

if the act could banish the feel of pressure, the terror of not being able to draw a deep breath.

A knock on the driver window ripped a new scream from her, but she gasped in relief as she saw Sheriff Tom Grayson standing next to her car. He'd either heard the horn from his office down the street or somebody had called and he'd come to investigate.

A new torrent of tears escaped her as she unlocked the car and opened the door. "He tried to kill me," she finally managed to gasp as she nearly tumbled out of the car. Her throat burned and her words sounded raspy.

"Who?" Tom asked as he grabbed her arm to steady her trembling stance.

"I don't know who. I didn't see his face. He was hiding in the backseat of my car." She raised a hand to her throat. "He…he tried to choke me. I hit him with my high heel and when I leaned on the horn he ran out of the car."

Tom used his cell phone and called for his brother, Caleb. "Which way did he run?" he asked her as he clicked off the phone. In the distance Caleb left the sheriff's station down the street and hurried toward them.

"Back that way," she replied as she pointed down the street. Her heart banged against her ribs and the taste of horror crawled up the back of her aching throat.

Within minutes Caleb was chasing after the attacker and Tom was leading her down the block to the warm interior of the sheriff's office. Once inside he deposited her into a chair in his office and instructed Deputy Sam McCain to get her a cup of coffee.

Layla glanced at the clock above Tom's desk and realized it had only been about fifteen minutes since she'd left her office to get into her car to go home.

It felt like an eternity. It felt like a nightmare and no matter how hard she tried she couldn't wake up. Somebody had tried to kill her. Somebody had tried to kill her. The words thundered in her head over and over again.

She took the coffee from Sam not because she wanted to drink it but rather because she needed the warmth to banish the chill that gripped her.

"Tell me exactly what happened," Tom said.

"There's not much to tell," she said, surprised when a laugh escaped her. Hysterical. She was definitely on the verge of becoming hysterical.

She took a sip of the coffee and leaned back against the hard surface of the chair back. "I got into the car, he wrapped his arm around my neck and he squeezed."

"Was your car locked?"

"Yes. At least I think it was but maybe not. I looked around to make sure nobody dangerous was lurking when I left the office and I didn't think about anyone hiding in my backseat."

"Did he say anything?"

She shook her head. "The only sound he made was a grunt when I hit him with my shoe. I hope I didn't break the heel when I smashed him. Those shoes were expensive." Once again a nervous burst of laughter rose to her lips but she quickly swallowed it down.

It was a fault of hers, the inexplicable need to make light when she was scared or upset. "Why would somebody do that to me, Tom? Why would somebody try to hurt me?"

He frowned thoughtfully. "Can you think of anyone in your personal life who might be angry with you?"

"No, nobody," she said firmly. "You know me, Tom. I don't make enemies."

"What about professionally? Any problems at the office?"

"I'm a Realtor, for goodness' sake. I work for myself and I make people happy." She set the cup on the edge of the desk with trembling fingers.

At that moment Caleb returned to the office. "I didn't see any sign of anyone, but I did a cursory check of the car and grabbed your purse," he said to Layla. He handed her the oversize bag and then turned to Tom. "I also found this in the backseat." He held up a plastic bag with a syringe in it.

"Oh, my God, what's that?" Layla asked as a new horror washed over her. "That's not mine," she exclaimed. "I don't do drugs of any kind."

"I don't know what's in it, but it looks fully loaded," Caleb replied.

Tom rose from his chair and motioned Caleb out of the room. "Excuse us for just a minute," he said as he and Caleb walked out into the hallway.

Left alone, Layla's anxiety flew off the charts as she grappled with what had just happened to her. She couldn't imagine anyone hating her enough to try to strangle her. She even got along well with her ex-boyfriends.

Sure, she knew that a lot of people in town thought she was shallow and superficial, brash and a bit of a wise-mouth. She also knew that there were some who probably thought she was a bit loose, but Layla was the first to admit that she made a lot of mistakes when it came to men.

Even as she thought about her personal life she knew the truth, and the truth was far more terrifying than an ex-boyfriend.

She reached for the cup and took another sip of the coffee, but the warmth of the brew didn't begin to touch the chill that had taken up residency in her bones.

What happened now? Did she just get into her car and go home? The idea of being alone in her house terrified her. What if he knew where she lived? What if he came back to finish the job?

Other women had recently disappeared in the town of Black Rock. A new chill took possession of her body at this thought. They'd disappeared and never been seen again.

Tom returned to the room and sat at his desk, a sober expression on his handsome face. "Layla, you know about the missing women we've had in the last couple of months."

"Of course," she replied. "I was just thinking about

that." There had been four women who had disappeared from Black Rock in the last four months or so, including Tom's own sister, Deputy Brittany Grayson. "It was him, wasn't it?" Her heart beat so fast she felt slightly nauseous. This was the truth she hadn't wanted to think about.

Tom nodded. "Caleb and I think maybe it's possible you were intended to be number five."

His words hung in the air between them as she stared at him in horror. Nobody knew what had happened to the women who had disappeared but the general opinion of everyone in town was that they were all dead.

"We think that all the women were taken from their cars. Most people don't look in their backseats when they get behind the wheel. I would guess that the syringe is filled with something that would knock a person unconscious. He was probably going to choke you unconscious and then administer the drug."

"Or it could have killed me instantly," she said. Her throat began to hurt again, as if in response to their conversation.

He hesitated a moment, his eyes flashing darkly. "We'll know more about that after we send it to the lab."

"So, what happens now?" she finally managed to ask.

"As terrible as this experience has been for you, this could be the break we've been waiting for. We're keeping your car and will go through it with a fine-tooth comb to see if the attacker left anything behind besides that syringe. Hopefully we'll get some hair or fiber or fingerprints that will lead us to an arrest."

"And what about me?" she asked.

"I've called Benjamin. He's going to come by and take you by your house to get some things then we're going to stash you in a cabin out at the ranch until we're certain you aren't in any danger."

"A cabin?" She didn't know about any cabin located on the Grayson property.

He nodded. "It's kind of a family secret, an old caretaker's cottage that my parents renovated years ago."

"What about my cat?"

Tom frowned. "You have a neighbor or somebody who can take care of him while you're gone for a couple of days? Either that or we can see if Larry Norwood can board him."

Layla set the coffee cup on the desk and then leaned back once again, finding it difficult to comprehend everything that was happening. "The only person I'd trust to take care of Mr. Whiskers is Portia and she's allergic." Portia Perez was Layla's best friend and Caleb's fiancée. "I guess it would be okay to board him for a couple of days. I'm sure Larry would take good care of him."

Larry Norwood was the town veterinarian and Layla was comforted by the fact that he seemed like a nice guy who loved animals. Mr. Whiskers already knew the vet, for Larry's office was where she took the cat for checkups and shots.

"I'll see that he's taken care of," Tom assured her. "The important thing is to get you someplace safe until we can figure out exactly what's going on." He leaned forward, his dark eyes piercing into her. "Layla, is there anything else you can tell me about the man who attacked you?"

She thought of those terrifying moments in the car when she'd been certain death was a mere heartbeat away. "Nothing," she finally replied. "It all happened so fast. All I can tell you is that he was strong."

"If you think of anything else, if you think of anyone who might have a reason to harm you, let me know. In the meantime all I need from you is that you tell nobody where we're putting you, and I mean nobody, and that you stay put until we know the danger has passed."

The idea of staying in a cabin alone was nerve-racking, but the thought of going back to her house all alone was absolutely terrifying. "If the culprit is who you think it is, then maybe he won't bother me again since I managed to get away."

"Maybe, or it's possible that he'll be more determined than ever to get to you."

A tiny laugh escaped her. "Thanks for the reassurance."

"I'm not going to waste my breath giving you false assurances," he replied. "There's no way to know if this is tied to the other disappearances or not. We don't have enough information right now to know what's going on. But, the one thing I don't want to do is minimize the possible danger." His mouth was set in a grim line. "I don't want to lose another woman in this town."

"I don't want to be the one you lose," she replied. "I know it's hard to believe coming from me, but I'll do whatever you tell me to do, Tom."

At that moment Benjamin appeared in the doorway. Benjamin was another of Tom's brothers who worked as a deputy, but rumor had it he intended to quit his deputy duties in the spring and focus on ranching and Edie Burnett, the new woman in his life.

"Layla, heard you've had a bit of a rough night," he said.

She forced a smile. "That would be the understatement of the year."

"You ready to head out?"

She looked at Tom, who nodded his assent. "I'll be in touch to let you know what's going on. And don't worry about your cat. I'll see he gets to Norwood's later tonight or first thing in the morning."

She stood in an uneven stance minus one shoe. "Can I get my other high heel from the car?" she asked.

"It's evidence," Tom replied. "I'm hoping that if you managed to hit him and break some skin then we might have some DNA on the shoe."

She took off the shoe she still wore and then looked at Benjamin. "Then I guess I'm ready to go." A new burst of fear swept through her as she realized she wasn't going home to Mr. Whiskers and her own bed, but rather was in effect going into protective custody.

It took only ten minutes for Benjamin to get her from the sheriff's office to her small house. She'd always felt safe in the three-bedroom ranch house she'd bought five years before. But she didn't feel safe now. The shadows in the rooms suddenly felt ominous and she jumped at every ordinary noise. She was grateful to have Benjamin with her.

She packed a large suitcase of the things she considered essential, kissed Mr. Whiskers goodbye and then they were back in Benjamin's truck and on their way to his ranch.

The adrenaline that had pumped through her from the moment the arm had wrapped around her neck eased away, leaving a gnawing fear that had her shaky.

"Please tell me this cabin has electricity," she said as she leaned forward to get the benefit of the warmth blowing from the heater vents.

Benjamin smiled. "Electricity, running water and cable television," he replied. The smile faltered somewhat. "There's something else you need to know. Jacob is staying at the cabin."

Shock waves shot through her. "Jacob? But, I thought he was in Kansas City working for the FBI." As far as Layla was concerned Jacob had always been the hottest of the Grayson men. She'd had a major crush on him before he'd left town to become an FBI agent.

"He was, but he's been back for about six months and staying in the cabin."

"Did he get hurt or something?"

"Or something," Benjamin replied. "He hasn't told any of us what brought him back, but he's not the same man he was when he left Black Rock. Anyway, I just thought I should let you know that you'll be sharing the space with him."

Layla leaned back and digested this new information. At least she'd have some company and it didn't hurt that her company was a man who had always intrigued her. "I'm sure we'll get along just fine," she said. It also didn't hurt that her protective custody involved an FBI agent.

"Good luck with that," Benjamin muttered under his breath as he turned into the entrance of his ranch.

They drove past the ranch house and across the pasture. "How's Edie?" she asked.

A smile flashed across Benjamin's face. "Terrific."

Edie Burnett had come to town to check on the well-being of her grandfather, Walt Tolliver. She and Benjamin had fallen hard for each other and Edie had moved in with him.

A fist of loneliness slammed Layla in the stomach. It wasn't an unfamiliar punch. Sometimes she thought that she'd been born lonely and that she'd never find somebody who might help ease that affliction.

It certainly wasn't from lack of trying. She felt as if she'd dated every eligible bachelor in Black Rock between the age of twenty-one and forty.

She shook her head, wondering if she was losing her mind. Somebody had just tried to kidnap or kill her and she was thinking about her love life. Because that's not scary to think about, she told herself, because that didn't fill her soul with terror.

They drove over a rise and in the beams of the headlights in the distance she saw the small cabin nearly hidden by evergreen trees crowding in on every side.

A faint light glowed at the front window, but it didn't add any sense of real welcome to the isolated place. The front porch was bare and the exterior paint was starting to show signs of age.

"You'll be safe here. Few people even know this cabin exists," Benjamin said as he parked the truck in front of the small structure and turned off the engine.

Layla got out of the truck, a bit unsteady on the uneven ground in the red high heels she'd put on at her house. With her tight jeans and in a new red sweater she felt ready to face whatever life threw at her.

Benjamin grabbed her oversize suitcase from the back of his truck and together they walked up the stairs to the small porch and the front door.

Benjamin knocked and a deep voice replied. He opened the door and Layla stepped inside. Her first impression was that the place was downright cozy with a fire crackling merrily in the stone fireplace and a thick throw rug covering an expanse of the gleaming hardwood floor.

"What in the hell is she doing here?" The deep voice

came from a recliner and a stunned surprise fluttered through her as she got her first glimpse of Jacob Grayson.

His dark hair hung almost to his shoulders and his jaw was covered with a thick growth of whiskers. She could tell from the hollows in his cheeks that he'd lost weight, but his shoulders were still broad beneath the navy sweater he wore and his jeans hugged the length of his long legs.

It was his eyes that made her breath catch in her throat. Dark as night and filled with the shadows of hell, they bore into her with intensity. He looked at her, her suitcase and then at Benjamin. "What the hell is going on here?"

A bubble of laughter unintentionally escaped her. "I guess you didn't get the memo," she said. "I'm your new roomie."

Chapter 2

Jacob recognized her immediately even though the last time he'd seen her Layla West had been about nineteen years old. Even back then she'd liked her jeans tight and her heels high and it looked as if nothing had changed. She'd be about twenty-eight now, definitely not a kid anymore.

There was some small part of his brain that processed the scent of her sexy perfume in the air, part of him that was drawn to the shine of her long blond hair, but the bigger part of his brain stared at Benjamin through angry narrowed eyes.

It would be just like his well-meaning brothers to set up something like this in an effort to pull him from his self-imposed isolation. Nothing like a hot, sexy woman to pull a man back into life. *Yeah, right,* he thought bitterly.

"Is this some kind of a joke because if it is I'm not laughing." What he wanted to do was shove both Benjamin and the lovely Layla West right back out the door. Instead he got out of the chair and approached where Benjamin stood.

"Of course you're not laughing," Benjamin replied tightly. "That might make you human." He dropped Layla's suitcase on the floor and looked at her. "Layla, would you excuse us for a minute?"

He grabbed Jacob's arm and pulled him toward the door. The two men stepped out on the porch and into the cold night air. "This is not a joke," Benjamin said, a touch of uncharacteristic anger in his voice. "This isn't about you and any issues you might have, Jacob. We've all pretty much left you alone out here for the last six months. We've asked damn little of you and hoped to hell you'd pull yourself together."

The cold December wind sliced through Jacob's sweater almost as effectively as the disgust in his younger brother's voice. He jammed his hands into his pockets and waited for Benjamin to finish whatever it was he wanted to say.

"Layla was attacked this evening when she got into her car after work. She managed to get away but she didn't see who was responsible. We need to stash her someplace where nobody will know where she is for a day or two while we figure out what's going on."

"Why don't you put her at your place? You could hide her there. Edie doesn't strike me as the loose-lipped kind of woman." Edie and Benjamin lived at the ranch house up the lane.

"Edie isn't, but you know Walt. He means well but he has never met a secret he could keep." Benjamin jammed his hands into his coat pockets.

Jacob sighed, knowing his brother was right. Walt Tolliver was Edie's grandfather, a nice old man who had become something of a local hero after being responsible for bringing to light a scheme involving illegal experiments on the dead of Black Rock. Walt meant well, but Benjamin was right, the old man had never met a secret he could keep.

"A couple of days at the most," Benjamin said. "Surely you can force yourself to be civil for that long."

Maybe he could pretend she wasn't there for that length of time, Jacob thought to himself. "Whatever," he finally said, the cold seeping deep into his bones.

He stepped back in the door where Layla stood poised for flight next to her suitcase.

"Take off your coat. Relax, you're staying," he said grudgingly as he threw himself back into the recliner where he'd been seated before they'd arrived.

"Great, this should be fun," she said with a touch of sarcasm. She took off her coat and draped it over her arm. "Where do you want me to put my things?"

"There's only one bedroom," Benjamin said. "I'm

sure my brother would want you to have it." He pointed
to one of the doors off the main room.

Layla looked at Jacob as if to see if that was okay. He
nodded. Most nights he slept in the recliner or on the
sofa anyway. Besides, if he was lucky she'd stay in the
bedroom and out of his hair until Benjamin came back
to retrieve her.

"We'll stay in touch," Benjamin said to Layla as he
backed toward the front door. "You'll be safe here, Layla.
Just give me a call if you need anything."

With that, Benjamin left. Jacob picked up the remote
control to the television and turned the volume up enough
that conversation would be difficult. He knew it was rude
and he didn't care.

He'd stopped caring about anything six months ago
when he'd left his job in Kansas City with the FBI and
had returned to Black Rock and this cabin. All he wanted
was to be left alone with the crushing guilt that never left
him and the images of dead women that haunted him.

"I guess I'll just get settled in," she said, raising her
voice to be heard above the television.

He watched as she pulled the suitcase toward the
bedroom, unable to help but notice how her jeans cupped
her curvy behind. As she disappeared into the bedroom
he got up and grabbed a beer from the fridge.

In the past six months beer had become his best
friend. Although he never got falling-down drunk, he
drank just enough to dull his senses and aid in a little
selective amnesia.

Hopefully it would take her at least an hour to unpack that suitcase, which had looked big enough to hold a month's worth of clothes, and hopefully she'd only be in his personal space long enough to wear one of the outfits she'd packed.

He took a long pull on the fresh beer and tried to ignore the scent of her that still eddied in the air. He couldn't remember the last time he'd smelled the pleasant scent of a woman or touched warm silky skin in a fevered caress.

The only women in his life in the last year had initially been faces on flyers who had eventually become bodies in crime scene photos. And their deaths had been his fault.

He shook his head and took another deep swallow of his beer to dispel any horrible visions that might drag across his brain. He didn't want to think about those women, knew that dwelling on them would cast him into the darkest of despair.

As if this personal baggage wasn't enough, his sister had disappeared almost four months before. He'd used what resources he could in an attempt to find any trace of her whereabouts, but had come up empty-handed, as was the case in all his brothers' investigations.

He had a feeling his sister was dead, otherwise they would have found something, heard something by now. It was just a new grief he refused to acknowledge.

He frowned as Layla emerged from the bedroom and sat on the sofa. He glanced at her and she gave him an overly bright smile. "So, what are you doing here? Are you in hiding, too?" she asked.

"Something like that," he replied. The red sweater she wore enhanced the pale blond of her hair and the blue of her eyes. Suddenly his thoughts turned to another woman. Sarah. She'd been wearing red the last time he'd seen her. His stomach clenched tight.

"I usually hear all the gossip but I haven't heard anyone mention that you were back in town." Her voice was raised to be heard over the blaring television.

Reluctantly he lowered the volume. "Besides my family I'd prefer nobody know I'm here."

"Why?"

"Because I want it that way," he replied curtly and hoped she'd drop the subject. He didn't intend to tell anyone what had brought him back here, the culpability he'd had in the last case he'd worked.

She crossed one long slender leg over the other and leaned back, looking as comfortable as if she were in her own home. "So, what do you do to pass the time?"

He sighed. She was obviously determined to have some sort of conversation with him. "I drink beer and watch television or I listen to the silence," he replied pointedly.

"I've never been a beer drinker. I like wine, especially a light blush, and sometimes a strawberry daiquiri is good. But if I'm celebrating something special I love a glass or two of champagne."

Shoot me now, Jacob thought as she continued explaining what drinks she liked and didn't like. She certainly didn't act like a woman whose life had just been threatened. It was just his luck to be cooped up with a superficial woman hell-bent on talking him to death.

When she finally wound down her alcoholic drinks speech, she launched into a monologue about how much she liked Christmas. He tuned her out, making her voice white noise in his head.

"Jacob?"

He reluctantly tuned back in as he realized she must have said his name several times. "Is there anything around here to eat?" she asked. "I skipped dinner and now I'm starving."

He pointed toward the kitchen. "Help yourself." He breathed a sigh of relief as she got up and disappeared into the next room.

There had been a time when he liked nothing more than sitting with an attractive woman and indulging in a little flirtatious small talk, and if it led to something more all the better. But, that had been before Sarah, and before the case that had broken him.

And he was broken.

As an FBI agent.

As a man.

He took another long pull of his beer as he listened to the sounds of rattling pots and pans from the kitchen. Benjamin always made sure he had plenty of groceries so she'd have any number of things to choose to eat.

His stomach rumbled as the scent of frying bacon filled the air. He hadn't eaten supper and he'd skipped lunch, as well, opting for a liquid diet of booze.

Most of the time if he was going to eat he either made himself a sandwich or zapped something in the microwave. Food had lost its appeal, as had most things in life.

Layla stepped into the doorway. "I'm making a bacon and cheese omelet. Want half?"

He didn't want anything from her, but his stomach decided otherwise and he nodded affirmatively. "Okay," he agreed. Within minutes she called to him that it was ready.

"I'll just eat in here," he replied.

Once again she appeared in the doorway. "No way," she said with a hint of steel in her voice. "I've got the food on the table and it's only civilized that we eat there."

"What makes you think I'm civilized?" he countered. God help him, not only did he have a chatty woman on his hands but apparently a bossy one, as well.

"If you want to eat, then you'll come into the kitchen." She disappeared from the doorway.

He stared after her. Who did she think she was to come in here and try to tell him what he should and shouldn't do? If she thought she was going to run this place while she was here then she had another thing coming. Reluctantly he got to his feet.

He was starving and at the moment the issue didn't seem important enough to fight about. He carried his beer bottle into the tiny kitchen where she'd set the small dinette table for two. He dumped the rest of his beer down the sink drain, tossed the bottle into the trash and then took the seat at the table across from her.

Above the scent of the bacon he could smell the ridiculously sexy fragrance of her perfume. Sitting this close to her he could see the gold flecks that sparked in her blue eyes as she gazed at him and to his stunned surprise a tiny flame ignited in the pit of his stomach.

"So, what happened to you?"

The question surprised him, along with his unexpected physical reaction to her nearness. "Nothing happened." He picked up his fork and focused on the food in front of him even though he felt her gaze remaining on him.

"You look like hell," she said.

Jacob set down his fork and gazed at her balefully. "We're here together through no choice of mine. I don't want to share personal feelings and experiences with you. I don't want to make pleasant little chitchat. I just want to be left alone." He picked up his fork and began to eat once again.

"Looks to me like you've been left alone too long," she said as if unable to not be the one who had the last word.

He ignored her and ate as quickly as possible, ignoring the fact that she continued to look at him as she ate her dinner. When he was finished he carried his dish to the sink, washed it and set it in the drainer to dry.

He left the kitchen without saying a word and returned

to the recliner that had become his second best friend, after his beer.

Within minutes she'd returned to the room and to his dismay once again positioned herself on the sofa. "So, Layla, what's been going on in your life for the last couple of years?" she said. "Oh, not much. I own the only realty in town but unfortunately business has been pretty slow lately. I like Chinese food, I'm a Libra and I love to dance."

For the first time in months Jacob felt the urge to smile. It stunned him. It felt like an affront to all the blood that stained his hands.

"Are you always so irritating?" he asked.

She frowned as if seriously considering his question. "I suppose it depends on who you talk to. My friends don't find me irritating, but it's possible some of my old boyfriends might. And just for the record you're more than a little bit irritating, too."

He felt her gaze on him as he stared at the television. "You didn't used to be this way," she continued. "In fact you used to be every teenage girl's fantasy."

"Yeah, well things change, and now I'm going to sleep." He clicked off the television, lowered his chair to a sleep position and then closed his eyes.

He was acutely aware of her in the silence of the room—her scent, the bubbling energy she brought and the faint whisper of the sound of her breathing. He felt her gaze on him but refused to open his eyes.

He breathed a sigh of relief as he heard her finally get

up, and a moment later the door to the bedroom closed. He opened his eyes and frowned thoughtfully.

She was going to be a pain in his ass. Beautiful and sexy, she was apparently a woman who was accustomed to getting her own way. Once again he told himself that she certainly didn't seem to be traumatized by the events of the night that had brought her here.

A day or two, that's what Benjamin had said to him. She just needed to be here for a short time. Surely Jacob could handle her presence for forty-eight hours or so.

He turned off the lamp on the end table and closed his eyes but visions of Layla instantly danced in his head. Even when she'd been nineteen and he'd been twenty-four and home for a visit, he'd been aware of her around town, but she'd been too young and he'd had his job in Kansas City and so he hadn't pursued anything with her.

And now she was all grown up and under his roof. Not that he cared, not that he intended to do anything about it. He had enough dead women in his mind. There wasn't room for a breathing one, no matter how sexy he found her. He just wanted her out of his space.

His head once again filled with thoughts of Sarah. He'd met her when he'd been twenty-six years old and she'd been twenty-four, and he'd fallen hard. She'd been beautiful and fun, bubbling with the same kind of energy that Layla possessed. She loved to talk, loved to dance and had stolen his heart almost immediately.

It had taken Jacob months to get up his courage to ask

her to marry him and when he finally had she'd laughed at him. She'd told him that she was far too young to get married, that she was just having fun and now that he'd gotten so serious about her it wasn't going to be fun anymore.

That had been the last time he'd seen Sarah and his last attempt at a relationship with anyone. She'd devastated him and he never wanted to feel that way again about anyone.

He must have fallen asleep for the scream awakened him. He jerked up, disoriented for a moment as he realized the scream hadn't been one of his own that occasionally woke him from a nightmare.

The fire had burned down to hot coals and the room had grown chilly. He reached out and turned on the lamp next to him. The sound came again, a sharp, piercing scream that sliced through him.

Layla! Full consciousness slammed into him as he recognized her scream. Had the person who had tried to harm her earlier in the evening found her again?

He fumbled in the drawer in the end table and pulled out his gun, then jumped out of the chair and raced toward the bedroom door, hoping—praying—that he wouldn't find yet another woman murdered on his watch.

"Layla, come out, come out, wherever you are."
The familiar voice shot terror through Layla, who was crouched beneath the old front porch.

"Come on, little girl. Take your punishment like a trouper."

Layla's breaths came in rapid, shallow gasps. Don't let him find me. Please don't let him find me. Her heart pounded in her chest so loud she was afraid he'd hear it. Maybe if she stayed hidden long enough he'd pass out and forget that he'd decided she needed a beating.

She screamed as a hand reached under the porch and grabbed her by the hair. Tears filled her eyes as her scalp burned and her body was dragged across the rocks and dirt.

She couldn't breathe.

Suddenly she was in her car and hands wrapped around her throat and squeezed unmercifully. He was killing her and Layla didn't want to die. She wanted to live and get married and have babies. She wanted to have lunch with her friends and be happy.

But she was dying, her throat being squeezed so hard no sweet air could reach her lungs. Inside her mind she screamed for help, but no sound escaped her lips. She knew nobody could help her. She was going to die alone—as she had been all her life.

"Layla!"

The deep voice cut through her, familiar and yet somehow frightening. She struck out with her fists, with her legs, desperate to get away from him, fighting for her very life.

"Hey, hey! Stop! Layla, wake up! It's Jacob."

She came awake with a gasp for air as her heart crashed in a frantic beat. She blinked against the brightness of the overhead light and then Jacob came into focus.

It was Jacob, not the man who had tried to kill her. It was Jacob, not her father who had been the source of so many of her nightmares.

Without thought, functioning only with need, she sat up and grabbed him around the neck, pulling him close as the residual fear from her nightmare shuddered through her body.

"You're okay," he said gruffly, not moving away but not engaged in the hug. "It was just a dream. You should be fine now."

She shook her head and burrowed her face into the crook of his neck where warmth and the faint scent of minty soap and a spicy cologne comforted her. The dream had been a horrifying blend of past and present and her heart still rocked in her chest with an unsteady rhythm.

He released a small sigh and finally wrapped his arms around her. She felt the strength of his arms and shoulders, the very warmth of him that radiated through his T-shirt and her silk nightgown. She closed her eyes and reveled in the moment of safety, of complete and total security.

Even as she began to fully relax she felt the tension that filled him. It was finally he who disentangled himself from her and stepped back, his eyes dark and enigmatic. "You'll be okay now," he said and turned and left the room.

Instantly she was chilled to the bone, bereft with the lack of his presence. She wrapped her arms around her own shoulders, seeking comfort as her mind raced with the images not only from her dream, but from her attack earlier in the evening.

Just go back to sleep, she told herself, but the idea of falling back into those same dreams was terrifying. What she needed was to talk about something, about anything that might take her mind off her dreams, off the fact that somebody had tried to kill her that night.

She eyed the doorway longingly, wanting to get out of the bedroom where she was alone with her thoughts. Jacob certainly wasn't the most sociable creature on the face of the earth, but at the moment he was all that she had.

Making a decision, she slid out of bed, pulled on the sleek, short robe that matched her leopard print nightgown and went into the living room.

She turned on the lamp next to Jacob's recliner and offered him a tentative smile. "I feel like talking. Do you mind?"

"Would it make a difference if I said yes?" One of his dark eyebrows rose sardonically.

"Probably not," she replied truthfully and sat on the sofa. "I can't go back to sleep right now. I'm afraid I'll go right back into that horrible nightmare. Can we just sit here and talk for a few minutes?"

She could tell he'd rather eat nails, but he gave her a weary nod and put his chair into the upright position. "You want to talk about your nightmare?"

"Absolutely not. That's the last thing I want to talk about." She fought against the race of a shiver that threatened to walk up her spine. "I just want to talk about pleasant things." He frowned, as if he couldn't imagine anything pleasant to discuss.

"So, what's your favorite food?" she asked, desperate to talk about something—anything—no matter how mundane.

"Pizza, anything Mexican and I like a good steak." He stared at the blank television screen. "What about you?"

"I think it would be easier for me to list the kinds of food I don't like. Brussels sprouts and lima beans. Other than those, I love almost everything."

He focused his gaze on her and she couldn't help but notice the quick slide from her face to the gaping top of her robe. His frown deepened as he once again jerked his attention back to the television screen.

An uncomfortable silence descended as Layla gathered her robe more closely around her. She knew she should go back to bed, but now she was afraid her dreams would be haunted by his dark gaze.

"What kind of television shows do you like to watch?" she asked in an effort to keep the conversation flowing. "Personally I love most of the sitcoms that are on now. There's nothing better than a good laugh after a day of work. I'm also a reality show freak. They're all so silly but they definitely take your mind off your own problems."

Once again he looked at her, a wry lift to his lips. "And what kind of problems do you have? Whether to buy the shoes you want today or wait to see if they go on sale tomorrow?"

There was a derisive edge to his voice that instantly rankled her. "That's right," she replied with a forced airiness. "I'm all about shopping and going out to lunch and good times." Her voice broke as a sudden wash of emotion gripped her. "I'm sure that's why somebody hid in the backseat of my car tonight and tried to choke me to death."

He cursed silently under his breath. "I'm sorry, that was uncalled for. I've obviously lost my social skills while I've been cooped up here."

He offered her a smile and in that gesture she remembered the man she'd once had a major crush on. "I really don't know anything about you except that you said you owned the realty in town," he said.

She nodded. "I opened the business four years ago, just after my father died. I love finding the right home for my clients and business was good for about two years. But it's been lean lately." She began to relax as she thought about her work. "Hopefully the economy is turning around now and business will get better again."

"What about your mother? Where is she?" His gaze remained fixed on her face.

"She died when I was seven." And that was when all the love in Layla's life had also disappeared. A wave of grief tried to pull her into its clutches, but she fought it, refusing to go there.

"And you don't have any brothers or sisters?"

"No, it was just me. You're lucky to have such a big family. It must be nice to have people who care about you," she replied.

"It has its moments, but it can also be a pain."

"Are you still with the FBI?"

The smile instantly disappeared, as if it had only been a figment of her imagination. "I'm retired."

She looked at him in surprise. "You're awfully young to be retired. What are your plans for the future?"

"To get some sleep before morning comes." His voice was clipped, filled with a new irritation as he reclined his chair once again. Layla knew the moment of tenuous peace and conversation between them was over.

"Then I guess I'll just say good night." She got up from the sofa, turned off the lamp next to him and then went back into the bedroom.

The bedroom was small, the double bed covered with what appeared to be a handmade patchwork quilt. A dresser with a mirror stood against one wall and a nightstand was against the bed.

It was a nice room and there was a photo of the entire

Grayson family hanging on the wall next to the dresser. She moved over to it and studied it.

Mr. and Mrs. Grayson stood together, looking happy and in love. They were dead now, killed in an airplane crash that had left their adult children alone.

The Grayson children all shared the trait of rich dark hair. Jacob stood with his arm around his sister, that charming devilish grin lifting his lips. All the Grayson men were drop-dead gorgeous, but they were also known as men who had humor in their eyes and a flirtatious smile on their faces.

Where was Brittany now? And where were the other women who had disappeared? There had been some speculation that one of the women had simply left town, but the others had seemingly vanished into thin air.

She moved away from the picture and turned off the bedroom light. Instead of getting into bed she moved to the window. It was a perfectly clear night, the moon a gigantic silver orb in the sky.

Her thoughts were momentarily consumed by the man in the next room. What had happened to Jacob Grayson? What had brought him to this cabin, living like a hermit with dark shadows bruising his eyes?

Something had happened to Jacob, something terrible, and she couldn't help but be intrigued. She also couldn't help but remember those brief moments when he'd held her in his arms. It had felt so safe and yet had held just a little bit of dangerous attraction.

And somebody out there in the darkness tried to kill

you tonight. Once again the reality of what had happened slammed into her.

As she finally climbed back into bed, she prayed whoever it was wouldn't find her again.

Brittany Grayson awoke suddenly, her heart beating frantically. She remained unmoving on the cot, eyes open to the utter darkness that claimed the shed or whatever structure they were held in.

How many days had it been? How many weeks or months? She'd lost track of the time that she'd been held captive. There were now four of them, four women held in jail-like cells. The last one had been brought in earlier in the week. Casey Teasdale had hung over her captor's shoulder like a sack of potatoes as he'd carried her in and placed her on the cot in the fourth cell.

"Almost time," he said to Brittany as he'd locked the door to assure Casey's imprisonment. The ski mask he wore effectively hid all his features, making it impossible for Brittany to identify him.

He gestured toward the empty cell. "One more and then the real fun begins, and I've got a special woman in mind to fill that one. A pretty blonde who is a bit feisty and managed to escape me once. She won't escape the next time."

He'd whistled as he'd strolled out of the shed, leaving her with a chill that had nothing to do with the temperature of the building. *One more and then the real fun begins.*

One woman taken was a crime. Two had been a pattern and three made him a serial offender, but four was a collection. The monster who held them was collecting them like fancy figurines and she had a feeling once his collection was complete he'd take great pleasure in smashing his figurines.

She sat up, unsurprised to hear Jennifer's sobs. Jennifer Hightower had been crying off and on since the moment she'd arrived.

Say something to comfort her, a small voice whispered inside Brittany's head. But, as she reached inside herself for the right words she realized she had no more comfort to give.

For the first time since she'd been kidnapped she was without hope, her very soul had been depleted.

Initially she'd been so sure that her brothers would find her. She knew they'd move heaven and earth to find out what had happened to her. But with each day that had passed without rescue, her fear had grown stronger and now it was screaming like a banshee in her head.

Enough time had passed since her disappearance that her brothers probably thought she was already dead. Maybe they'd even stopped looking for her. She lay back down on the cot and squeezed her eyes closed. No, they wouldn't stop looking, but she'd lost the hope that they might find her in time.

One more and then the real fun begins.

She knew in her gut that the real fun meant death to all the women that were in the cells.

Chapter 3

Dawn was just beginning to break when Jacob awakened. Instantly his head filled with a vision of Layla. When he'd burst into her room the night before in response to her screaming, he'd been ready to protect her with his life.

As he'd seen her in the bed, the sheet at her waist and the top of the sleek animal print nightgown barely covering her full breasts, a fist of desire had slammed into his gut. When she'd awakened and pulled him into an embrace, that fist had punched him over and over again as he'd held her in his arms.

He now got up from the recliner and threw a log and some kindling on the hot coals from the night before. Once the fire was blazing nicely, he decided a shower and a change in his thoughts were in order. Stepping into the bathroom he caught his reflection in the mirror above the sink.

You look like hell.

Layla was right. He did look like hell. He scraped a hand across his whiskered chin and then turned away from the mirror in disgust.

Half an hour later he left the bathroom clean-shaven and dressed in a freshly laundered navy turtleneck shirt and jeans. He made coffee, then carried a cup to the living room window and stared outside, his thoughts still on the woman who slept in the next room.

She was so full of life and seemed determined to bring him out of his isolation by talking him to death. She probably had dozens of men lined up waiting to spend time with her.

And somebody had tried to kill her.

He turned away from the window and wished he'd been paying more attention to what was going on in town. He knew his sister and somebody else had gone missing, but whenever his brothers had talked about it, he'd tuned it out, preferring his own drama to theirs. Now he wished he'd listened more carefully to them.

He glanced at the closed bedroom door and wondered how late she would sleep. Not that he cared. As long as she was sleeping she wasn't talking.

She reminded him of Sarah and that was a time in his life he didn't want to remember, a time when he'd had hopes and dreams and everything had seemed possible.

When Sarah had walked away from him she'd stolen his dreams. The final case in his career had shattered his hope.

It was just before nine when Layla finally emerged. Clad in her nightgown and a short matching robe and her hair sleep-tousled around her head, she gave him a heavy-lidded glance and a quick smile. "Coffee, then shower," she said as she disappeared into the kitchen.

His stomach muscles knotted with a tension he recognized. It surprised him that the first real emotion he'd felt for so long was lust. Her long slender legs had looked sleek and sexy beneath the short robe and he hadn't forgotten how her full breasts had looked spilling over the top of her nightgown the night before.

He'd assumed she'd grab a cup of coffee and then join him in the living room, but as several minutes went by he realized she wasn't coming out of the kitchen.

Leave her be, he told himself. After all, that's what he wanted from her. He should be enjoying the fact that she was awake and not talking to him.

Before he realized what he was doing he was on his feet and headed into the kitchen. She sat at the table, her dainty fingers wrapped around a stone coffee mug and her eyelids still lazy with sleep.

"You're obviously not a morning person," he observed as he refilled his own coffee cup. He sat across from her at the table, wondering what in the hell he was doing.

Her face wore a slightly pouty expression that he found oddly charming. "Mornings should be banned," she said, then lifted the coffee mug to her lips. She took a sip and eyed him over the rim of the cup. "Nice to see you have a chin beneath all that hair."

He rubbed a hand across his smooth jaw. "It was starting to bug me," he replied. The last thing he wanted her to think was that he'd shaved for her.

"You have a nice chin. You shouldn't hide it under all those whiskers." She took another sip of her coffee and then lowered the mug to the table. "Did you sleep well?"

"As well as I always do." There was no way he'd share with her the kind of nightmare images that haunted his dreams. "What about you? Any more bad dreams?"

"No. Thankfully I slept like a baby once I finally went back to sleep. Is there a phone in the house? I left my cell phone at my office last night and I need to call Tom to see if he took care of the favorite man in my life," she said.

"The man in your life?" He shouldn't be surprised that she had a boyfriend. What did surprise him was the unexpected sharp edge of disappointment that stabbed him. What was that all about? He sure as hell didn't want anything from her.

"Yeah, he's sixteen pounds of calico fur and his name is Mr. Whiskers."

"Any men of the human variety in your life?" he asked.

"Passing ships, not that I care." She lifted her chin slightly as if in defense of whatever he might say. "What about you? Is there some woman pining for you back in Kansas City?"

"Nope, I was too devoted to my work to have any real relationships." It was the easiest way to reply and it was somewhat the truth. After Sarah he hadn't wanted anything that might somehow involve his heart. "I'm not a relationship kind of man."

He could tell Layla wanted to ask him questions about what had happened in his work, about what had brought him back here, questions that he didn't want to answer. He stood and motioned to the old harvest gold phone hanging on the wall. "Feel free to make whatever calls you need. Just remember you aren't supposed to tell anyone you're here."

He got up and left her alone in the kitchen. He told himself it was so she could make her call in private, but the truth was something about Layla West had him off balance.

From the moment she'd breezed into the place the night before she'd brought a spark of life that had been missing. He felt the spark deep in his soul and he wasn't sure whether he liked it or not.

For the last six months he'd been immersed in his self-imposed isolation, bitter with memories and drowning in guilt and remorse. He didn't want to be rescued from himself by anyone.

He'd just gotten settled back into the recliner when she came out of the kitchen. "Mr. Whiskers is now in the care of Larry Norwood, so all is right in my world, and I'm going to take a shower."

The minute she disappeared into the bathroom Jacob was visited by images of her naked body standing beneath a steamy spray of water. He closed his eyes as he imagined the slide of the soap down the hollow of her throat, across her delicate collarbone and then on to her full breasts.

He could easily imagine himself stepping into that spray of water next to her and taking her into his arms. A vision of their hot soapy bodies sliding together tensed all the muscles in his stomach.

He jerked out of the fantasy as his cell phone rang. He pulled it from his pocket and saw from the caller ID that it was his brother, Tom.

"I just talked to Layla and she didn't sound too worse for the wear so I figured I'd better check in with you and see how it's going."

"It's going," Jacob replied, irritated by where he'd allowed his fantasy to take him. "You have any clues as to who attacked her?" Hopefully the crime would be solved and Layla could get out of here.

"Nothing. I was hoping to get some DNA off the shoe she used to whack him with, but we'll have to wait to see what comes back from the lab. Same thing with the hypodermic needle the perp dropped."

Jacob felt as if he'd entered an alternate universe. Layla hadn't mentioned anything to him about hitting her attacker with a shoe or a needle being involved. "Whoa, take it from the top. Layla didn't tell me much about the attack on her."

There was a moment of silence. "Are we talking about the same Layla West? Usually Layla tells anyone who will listen whatever crosses her mind. I imagine you shut her down before she could say much of anything about it to you."

Tom was right. Jacob had made it clear to Layla the night before that he didn't want to talk, that all he wanted was for her to shut up and go to bed. A sliver of shame worked through him.

As he listened to Tom relating the details of the attack, a grudging admiration for his roommate filled him.

She'd fought back. It sounded like she hadn't panicked, but rather had fought back using whatever resources she had at her disposal, in this case her shoe.

Even though she'd acted unconcerned about the attack, it was obvious from her nightmare that she'd been affected more than he'd initially thought.

"When you get a chance, I'd like to sit down with you and hear about these cases you're working on," Jacob said. He could tell he surprised Tom by the moment of stunned silence that followed.

"I'd like that," Tom finally replied. "Maybe a pair of fresh eyes will see something that we've all missed. You want to come here or meet me someplace else?"

Jacob still wasn't ready for his presence in town to be known. "Why don't we meet this evening after dinner at the big house? I'm sure Benjamin and Edie won't mind."

"I'll check with Benjamin and set it up. I'll bring Peyton and Lilly along. The women can chat while we talk."

"Sounds like a plan," Jacob agreed. "Then unless I hear something different from you, I'll see you this evening about seven."

The men hung up and by the time Jacob had poured himself another cup of coffee and settled back in his recliner, Layla was out of the bathroom. She was clad in a pair of jeans and a royal blue sweater that did amazing things to her eyes.

"Now I feel more human," she said as she sat on the sofa.

As he told her about the meeting with Tom that evening her lips curved in a happy smile. "I adore Peyton and little Lilly and I've been looking forward to getting to know Edie better. This will be a perfect opportunity."

Peyton and her daughter had been relative newcomers to Black Rock when Peyton's daughter, Lilly, had been kidnapped. As Sheriff, Tom had been on the case and when Lilly was found alive and well, the two had realized they'd fallen in love.

All of Jacob's brothers had found the loves of their lives, although none of them had married yet. They all were waiting for Brittany to return, a study in futility as far as Jacob was concerned.

"How about some pancakes?" Layla asked as she got up from the sofa.

"I'm really not hungry," he replied.

"Nonsense. Didn't anyone ever tell you breakfast is the most important meal of the day?" She flashed him a bright smile and then disappeared into the kitchen.

Jacob released a small sigh. There was no question that he had a strong physical attraction to Layla, but the last thing he wanted to do was follow up on it.

He didn't want to get involved with any woman; he still remembered too clearly the pain of Sarah's rejection. And if that wasn't enough he had a head full of dead women silently accusing him for botching their case, for being the impetus that had resulted in their murders.

He was a man meant to be alone and that's the way he liked it.

It was what he wanted.

.It was what he deserved.

Layla was grateful when it came time for them to leave for Benjamin's place. Jacob had been a bear all day, barely speaking to her and playing his television loud enough that the cows in the distant pasture had probably heard the noise.

There was a tension in the cabin that palpitated with its own energy. She wasn't used to being cooped up and after a single long day she was ready to scream. If Jacob had been living this way for the past six months it was no wonder he was half-mad.

She now gave herself a final check in the bathroom mirror and wondered if Caleb and Portia would also be at Benjamin's house. Portia Perez was dating Caleb Grayson and she was also Layla's best friend. Layla hadn't talked to Portia since she'd been attacked, although she was certain that Caleb had probably told her what had happened.

She and Portia talked to each other almost every day and at the moment Layla would love to see her friend and tell her about the horror of what had happened. She'd also like to whisper to Portia that despite his grumpy attitude, in spite of his brooding and downright rudeness, she was intensely drawn to Jacob Grayson.

"If that's not a heartbreak waiting to happen, then I don't know what is," she muttered to her reflection in the mirror. Not that she was a stranger to heartbreak, most of her relationships ended in that state.

She'd realized long ago that she was a woman who seemed to inspire great lust in men, but nothing deeper, nothing more lasting. She'd given up on finding true, long-lasting love a long time ago.

You aren't good for anything, girl. No man is ever gonna want you. Her father's voice thundered in her ears and she shook her head to cast it out.

From the time her mother had died when she was a child to the time of her father's death four years ago, she'd felt inadequate, lacking in any qualities that would make her worthwhile to anyone.

Her father had been a brutal man, both physically and

mentally abusive. "But you survived," she whispered to the woman in the mirror. "And you thwarted an attack by a madman."

"You going to be in there all night or are you ready to go?" Jacob's voice called from the other side of the bathroom door.

"I'm ready," she replied and left the bathroom. He stood by the front door, car keys in hand and a familiar scowl riding his features. She grabbed her coat and pulled it on, then gave him a bright smile. "What are we waiting for?"

He opened the door and they walked out into the cold night air. "Wait here," he said and then he walked off into the darkness of the night.

She stood on the porch, wondering where he had gone, but moments later a black pickup pulled up in front of the cabin with Jacob at the wheel.

"Where did this come from?" she asked as she slid into the passenger seat.

"There's a shed not far from here. I figured there was no way you could walk the distance to the house in those shoes."

She glanced down at her blue pumps and then looked at him. "You'd be surprised what I can accomplish in a pair of sexy high heels."

He grunted and pulled away from the cabin. It took only minutes to travel the lane that led to the big ranch house that had been the Grayson family home where Benjamin and Edie now lived.

All the lights were on, creating a welcoming glow as Jacob pulled up beside Tom's car. Edie greeted them at the door and ushered them inside as Benjamin's dog, Tiny, danced at their feet.

The house smelled of evergreen and cinnamon, and Christmas decorations adorned every available surface. Layla shoved aside a wistful twinge as she thought of the little tree she'd intended to unpack and put out the night she'd gotten attacked.

"The men are in the study and the ladies are in the kitchen," Edie said as she linked arms with Layla. "Come on, Layla. I've got chocolate cake and coffee and Peyton and I can't wait to chat with you."

As Edie pulled Layla toward the kitchen, she saw Jacob disappear into the next room with Tiny following close behind him.

The minute Layla entered the kitchen and saw Peyton with her daughter, nine-month-old Lilly, on her lap, Layla's heart swelled with a new wistfulness she rarely allowed herself to feel.

"La-La," Lilly said at the sight of Layla. She squealed in delight and held out her chubby little arms for Layla to take her.

"Lilly," Layla exclaimed as she scooped up the little girl and kissed her on her dimpled cheek. Lilly giggled and smacked her lips as if finding everything around her absolutely delicious.

"Here, I'll take her and you take off your coat," Peyton

said as she grabbed her daughter and returned to her chair at the table.

Layla slid out of her coat, which Edie took from her and hung on a hook near the back door. "That cake looks positively sinful," she said as she sat in the chair next to Peyton. "Are Caleb and Portia coming, too?"

"No, although Portia said to send you her love. Caleb is on duty tonight and she had something going at her daycare—a parents' night," Edie explained as she set a cup of coffee in front of Layla.

"Shouldn't you be there?" Layla asked Peyton. "Lilly goes to Portia's daycare."

"Tom and I decided to skip it." Peyton tucked a strand of her long blond hair behind her ear. "It's not every day Jacob emerges from his cave."

"How are things going there? I couldn't believe it when Benjamin told me he was putting you in the cabin with Jacob." Edie sat across from Layla.

"Yes, has he said anything to you about what brought him back here from Kansas City?" Peyton asked. "Tom has been so worried about him."

Layla shook her head. "No, nothing. He isn't the chattiest person in the world. I've only been there one night and a day and I already think there have been times when he'd gladly wring my neck."

She raised a hand to her throat as a flash of memory snapped through her—an arm wrapped around her throat, squeezing, choking her to death.

"Are you all right?" Edie reached across the table

and touched her hand, jerking her from the terror of that remembered moment. "You just went ghost pale."

"I'm fine," she replied with a forced smile of brightness. "I just...this has all been so crazy."

"Crazy scary," Peyton said. "Tom is beside himself trying to find out who is behind all the disappearances. He's not sleeping. He's barely eating and I've been worried sick about him."

"I just wish I would have paid more attention when I was attacked. I wish I would have twisted around enough to see who it was, or scratched his face enough that there would have been DNA under my fingernails," Layla said with frustration.

"You did what you were supposed to do, you survived the attack," Edie replied sympathetically.

"Yeah, but I just wish I could have survived the attack and identified the bad guy," Layla said.

She was grateful when the talk turned to more ordinary things, the forecast for snow in the next couple of days, the argument of which was better comfort food, chocolate cake or cookie dough ice cream.

As they ate cake and drank coffee, the conversation remained light and easy and Layla found it a relief from the tense air that had surrounded her all day in the cabin with Jacob. But it wasn't long before the conversation circled around back to Jacob.

"It has to be a woman," Peyton said as Edie picked up the cake plates from the table. "Somebody broke his heart badly and that's what brought him back here."

"I don't know, he doesn't seem to be the type to have much of a heart to break," Layla replied ruefully.

"Don't let that fool you." Edie returned to the table. "I think we can all agree that the Grayson men come off tough and immune to emotion, but if you dig deep enough you find a wealth of vulnerability."

"The tougher they are, the harder they fall," Peyton said with a nod of agreement.

"All I really know is that something bad happened to him, something that haunts him." Layla had seen the utter darkness in his eyes, but there had been a moment when he'd looked at her that she'd seen something else, something that had made her heart beat a little faster and her palms grow slightly damp. It had been a flash of naked hunger, a spark of want that had immediately been doused.

She had no illusions where Jacob was concerned and the last thing she needed in her life was another meaningless sexual encounter that would only leave her raw and bruised. Besides, he didn't even seem to like her very much.

"Earth to Layla." Edie's voice pulled her out of her inner thoughts and back to the conversation.

"Sorry, I drifted for a minute," Layla replied.

"I was just saying that I think nothing will be right with the Grayson men until they find out what happened to Brittany," Peyton said.

"Benjamin thinks she's dead." Edie whispered the words as if afraid to say them aloud.

"Tom refuses to accept that," Peyton replied. "He thinks as long as there is no body then there's hope. He wants her home for Christmas. That gives him less than three weeks to find her."

"There are a lot of places to hide bodies around Black Rock, places where nobody would find them," Layla said, fighting against a shiver that threatened to sweep over her.

She could have been one of the bodies left in the woods or buried out in some field. If she hadn't managed to hit her attacker with her shoe and scare him away, Peyton and Edie might have been sitting at this table wondering what had happened to her and speculating about where her body might be found.

The conversation was halted by the men coming into the kitchen. "Are you trying to keep that chocolate cake all to yourselves?" Benjamin asked as he placed a kiss on the top of Edie's head.

"You know how we women are about our chocolate," Peyton answered as she handed Lilly to Tom.

Layla watched Jacob, who stood slightly apart from his brothers. Whatever conversation the men had shared hadn't lifted the shadows in his eyes. If anything, they looked darker.

"Jacob, you ready for a piece of cake?" Edie asked as she got up from the table.

"No thanks, none for me," he replied.

"He's probably worried that a little bit of sugar might sweeten up his mood," Benjamin replied drily, then grunted in surprise as Edie elbowed him in the stomach.

At that moment the doorbell rang and Edie left the kitchen to answer it. She returned a moment later with Caleb in tow.

"What's up?" Tom asked, obviously surprised to see his little brother.

"I left the office to get a cup of coffee from the diner and when I came back I found this taped on the door." He held up an envelope with a gloved hand and looked at Jacob. "Somebody knows you're in town because it's addressed to Special Agent Jacob Grayson."

Jacob froze, his features not betraying a single emotion as he stared at the envelope. He made no move to reach for it and for a moment it was as if everyone was freeze-framed in a still photo.

"Open it," Jacob finally said, his voice deeper than usual.

Caleb nodded and opened the envelope and withdrew what appeared to be a plain white note card. "'Hello Agent Grayson,'" Caleb read aloud. "'Hope you've enjoyed your time off. I'm ready to play again. Are you?' It's signed 'The Professional' and there's a P.S. 'Brittany says to tell you hello.'"

Layla gasped aloud and looked at Jacob, who had gone sickly pale. He stumbled back a step, his mouth opening and closing as if he couldn't get enough air.

"No." The single word finally escaped him in a strangled whisper. Before anyone in the room could move or guess his intent he flew out of the kitchen and a moment later the front door slammed shut.

Nobody stirred as the roar of Jacob's truck filled the air. It was only when the sound drifted away that Tom looked at Layla. "Looks like you need a ride back to the cabin."

"What just happened? What does that note mean?" she asked.

Lilly began to cry, as if aware that something bad had just happened. Peyton comforted her while everyone looked at Tom.

Tom frowned. "I don't know what's going on, but Jacob obviously has some answers and I intend to stay in that cabin until he gives them to me. Sooner or later he'll have to show up there."

It was quickly decided that Benjamin would drive Peyton and Lilly home while Tom went to the cabin with Layla. As Layla got into Tom's car it was fear for Jacob that caused her heart to beat frantically.

That note had shaken him badly and she knew with certainty that Jacob wasn't a man who got shaken easily. Something bad was in the town of Black Rock and that bad had just reached out and touched Jacob Grayson.

And she knew with all her instincts, with all her heart and soul, that the bad had only just begun.

Chapter 4

Jacob roared out of the driveway that led onto the Grayson property and out on the highway. He slammed his foot down on the gas pedal as he clenched the steering wheel so tightly his knuckles were white.

Not again. The words screamed inside his head. He couldn't go through it all again. He *wouldn't* go through it all over again.

He reached out and flipped the heater fan on high, but he knew he'd never be warm again. The chill of pure evil had gripped him and would never let him go.

Eventually he eased back on his speed, not so much concerned for his own safety but for that of anyone he might meet on the road.

His thoughts raced. How had the bastard found him?

He'd been so careful to lay low. When he'd left Kansas City he hadn't told anyone where he was going. Only a handful of people knew he was back in Black Rock and he'd trust those people with his very life.

Maybe he didn't know for sure that Jacob was in Black Rock. Maybe it had just been a guess that Jacob had come home to the bosom of his family to lick his wounds.

This thought brought him little comfort. The madman was in Black Rock and, if his note was to be believed, he had Brittany in his grasp.

He wanted to stay in his truck and drive forever. He wanted to continue west until he reached California and drove into the ocean. But, he'd driven for twenty minutes when he finally turned the truck around and headed back toward the cabin.

Although he wished he could drive to the ends of the earth, he knew he had to go back. There was no way to escape, no matter how far he drove.

He had no intention of getting involved in a madman's game again, but Tom needed to know what he was up against. It was time for Jacob to let his brother know what had brought him home.

If Jacob had paid more attention to the crimes happening in Black Rock, to the disappearances of women over the last couple of months, he might have guessed sooner that The Professional was back at work.

Now there was no guessing. The Professional was

back and if they didn't find him then the women he held would die. His own sister would be killed.

But I can't do it again, he thought as he turned onto the Grayson property. He refused to be a part of the game a second time.

When he drove past Benjamin's house he noted that all the vehicles had disappeared from out front. Caleb would have probably gone back to the sheriff's office but he wasn't sure where Tom or Benjamin might have gone.

Layla. He hadn't even thought about her when he'd reeled out of the house. Surely somebody had taken her back to the cabin.

When he reached the cabin he had his answer. Tom's car was parked out front and he saw the slender silhouette of Layla watching from the front window.

For some reason, the sight of her standing there, as if anxiously awaiting his safe return, touched him. But any positive emotion he might have felt couldn't be sustained beneath the weight of what had happened, what he now knew to be true.

The Professional was back.

He turned off the truck engine but remained seated, dreading the idea of going inside and facing the demons that had been chasing him for the last six months.

Faces flashed before his eyes, the faces of the women he'd let down, women who had wound up dead because of him. Raw emotion churned in his stomach, making him feel half-nauseous.

When he finally did step into the cabin Tom was seated in his recliner and Layla rushed toward him, her eyes filled with concern. "Are you all right?" she asked anxiously.

He was surprised that it mattered to her, that she cared at all. He hadn't been particularly kind to her in the time they'd spent together. He reached out and touched her cheek, a gentle touch as he shook his head. "No, I'm not all right, but I'm here now."

"And you're going to tell me what's going on," Tom said, the familiar hint of steel in his deep voice.

Jacob nodded wearily and stepped away from Layla. He sank down on one end of the sofa while she sat on the other. He looked at his brother and for a long moment wasn't sure where to begin.

"Who is he?" Tom asked.

"A serial murderer," Jacob replied. His chest tightened painfully. "He contacted the FBI after he'd kidnapped three women in Kansas City. He gave us their names and the locations he'd taken them from. I was put in charge of the case and coordinated with the Kansas City Police Department." The words fell from his lips with the bitter taste of dread, of failure. "Everything he told us checked out so we knew he was the real deal."

He leaned back against the sofa cushion, as if the softness might alleviate the difficulty of talking about the events that had unfolded in that case.

"I don't know why he focused in on me, but he did," he continued. "He started calling me, taunting me with details of the kidnappings and the women he had in captivity. He told me what he was feeding them and how they all begged for their lives. He said he was taking care of their basic needs like the wicked witch who plumped up Hansel and Gretel before trying to cook them in her oven."

Neither Tom nor Layla said a word, but waited for him to continue. His thoughts reeled him back in time and his stomach knotted tight. "He alerted me when he took the fourth woman and said he had room for five. Told me that when he got his fifth victim it would be party time."

"Party time?" Layla finally spoke, her eyes huge and her pretty features unnaturally pale.

Jacob looked at her and frowned. "Maybe you should go into the bedroom while Tom and I talk."

Her chin lifted and her blue eyes narrowed. "Not a chance. If what we believe is true, then I was almost at one of his parties and I want to know everything."

Once again he was struck by the strength that shone from her eyes, a strength that radiated from the square set of her shoulders. Once again he realized there was definitely more to Layla West than her love of high-heeled shoes and her need to fill any silence with the sound of her own voice.

He looked back at Tom. "He called himself The Professional and his plan was that once he had five women he'd torture and kill them one by one. He fed not so much on the actual kills themselves, but rather on the terror of the women as they waited their turn to die."

"Dear God," Layla murmured softly.

"So, what happened?" Tom asked, a muscle knotting in his jaw line.

A blackness reached out to Jacob, the darkness of utter despair, of a pain too deep to acknowledge, too wide to endure. He clenched his hands in his lap and stared down at them as he was cast back to the past.

They'd interviewed hundreds of people, checked and double-checked family members and friends of the victims in an effort to find a connection that might lead them to the guilty party. But it had all been in vain.

"Jacob?" Tom softly prompted.

"We did everything we could to figure out who this man was, what his connection was to the victims, and we eventually came to the conclusion that it was random, there was no connection that we could find."

"And random makes things even more difficult," Tom said.

Jacob nodded. "Anyway, the story was picked up by a reporter and became a big deal," he continued. "These kidnapped victims weren't prostitutes or drug addicts, they were all from good families, young women with jobs and people who loved them. The press ate it up. Somebody leaked that I had personal contact with the perp and the reporters were all over me."

It had been a terrible time. He'd been eating, breathing and living the case. "I was exhausted, sick by the conversations I was having with the creep, suffering nightmares when I did finally manage to close my eyes. A reporter caught me at the wrong time and I snapped. I told him that the perp called himself The Professional but he was nothing special, just another garden-variety creep preying on helpless women."

He raised his head and looked at his brother, his heart beating a thousand miles a minute. "That night after the piece ran on the news The Professional called me. He was crazy with rage. He told me he was smarter than all of us, more cunning than any killer we'd ever chased. He promised to show me just how good he was and when he hung up I knew it was going to be bad."

Once again the darkness threatened to consume him. He got up from the sofa, unable to sit still as he finished the horrible story.

He picked up a log and threw it on the already hot flames in the fireplace, needing more warmth as he continued. "I got a call from him the next morning. He told me I'd pushed him over the edge, that he'd gotten his fifth victim and had his party and now he needed a little party cleanup crew."

Jacob turned and faced the fire and in the dancing flames he saw the faces of the women who had been depending on him to find them, the faces of the women he'd let down. He squeezed his eyes tightly closed, but the accusing faces refused to disappear.

The air in the cabin was suffocating and held an air of dreadful expectancy. Above the crackle of the fire he heard Tom shift positions in the recliner, felt Layla's gaze burning into his back.

"He gave me the address of an old abandoned warehouse in the river district of Kansas City. He said that if we hurried we might find them all still breathing. My team rushed to the location." He paused, the emotion he'd been fighting crawling up the back of his throat, constricting his chest to the point that he wasn't sure he could continue. He turned around and looked at his brother.

"And they were all dead," Tom said flatly.

Jacob nodded and drew in a deep breath. "They'd been tortured and killed sometime during the night. According to the coroner, there was as much as two hours between the first death and the last."

"Jacob, they were dead no matter what you did. You aren't responsible for what happened," Tom said, his gentle voice doing nothing to ease Jacob's torment.

"Don't you get it? If I hadn't shot off my mouth when I did then maybe we would have had more time," he exclaimed. "Maybe we would have been able to find those women before he killed them." A flash of anger swept through Jacob. It was so easy for somebody who had not been involved to attempt to absolve him of any guilt.

He sank down on the sofa once again and buried his face in his hands. For a long moment nobody spoke. Jacob's heartbeat thundered at his temples, making him feel sick to his stomach.

He finally raised his head and looked at Tom. "I'm not going through this again. I can't get involved with this. I came here so that I wouldn't be involved in any more crimes he might commit."

"According to the note you got, you are involved," Tom replied. "He knows you're here, Jacob."

Jacob shook his head. "He might know that I'm somewhere here in town, but he must not know that I'm here at the cabin. Otherwise that note would have been left here on my doorstep, a way to show his power and control." He shook his head more vehemently. "I'm not playing his game. I'll tell you what you need to know, what information we got before, but I'm out of this." Unable to stand himself or the situation another minute, he got up and went into the bathroom.

Once there he sluiced cold water over his face and dried off with a hand towel, refusing to look at his reflection in the mirror.

He threw the towel on the sink and then leaned against the door. He couldn't be responsible for what was going on now with The Professional. He couldn't be a part of it again. If he said something or did anything that resulted in more deaths, he'd never survive.

It was better to do nothing.

If he hadn't shot his mouth off to that damned reporter, if he hadn't belittled the killer, then maybe the murders wouldn't have happened when they did. Maybe he would have been able to glean more information from the phone calls he received from the man. Maybe...

maybe…maybe…all the maybes in the world didn't change what had happened.

He stayed in the bathroom until he could no longer hear any conversation going on in the living room, then he opened the door and walked out.

Layla was alone, seated on the sofa where she'd been when he'd exited the room. He didn't look at her but rather threw himself in the recliner and stared at the blank television screen.

"Tom said to tell you he'll call you first thing in the morning," she said.

He gave her a curt nod and then closed his eyes, as if he could shut out the world with a flip of his eyelids.

"Jacob, talk to me." Her voice was a soft plea. "Don't shut yourself off."

"Do me a favor and just leave me alone," he replied without opening his eyes.

Silence reigned for a moment and he wondered if maybe she'd gotten up and left the room. He cracked open an eyelid and saw her still seated on the sofa, her gaze lingering on him. He quickly snapped his eyelid closed once again.

"You can't keep yourself out of this," she said softly. "You can't hide anymore, Jacob."

He opened his eyes and glared at her. "What do you know about it? What do you know about anything? I can do whatever the hell I want to do. Just leave me the hell alone."

She got up from the sofa and walked to the side of

his chair. The scent of her perfume surrounded him as she leaned down to face him eye-to-eye. "I know that I think it's damned arrogant of you to believe that you and you alone were responsible for those women's deaths."

"I was," he half yelled.

"That's a bunch of nonsense," she retorted. "You didn't hold a gun to this Professional's head and force him to kidnap that last woman. You didn't force him to kill those women. It was his fault and nothing you said to that creep could have made a difference."

He wanted to tell her to shut up, that the last thing he needed or wanted from her was her input into the situation. He got up from the chair, not wanting her hovering over him. He stalked into the kitchen and opened the refrigerator door and grabbed a beer.

He was about to unscrew the top when she came into the kitchen. "Are you going to drink this away?" she asked. "Is that what you've been doing here for the last six months? How's that working for you, Jacob?"

"Don't push me, Layla," he warned. "Just back off and leave me alone."

With a stubborn glint in her eye, rather than doing as he asked she advanced toward him. "You've been left alone to wallow in your self-pity for too long."

She walked closer to him and when she was close enough to touch him she took the beer bottle from his hand and set it on the counter.

"I felt his arm around my neck, Jacob," she continued, her gaze steady and determined as it held his. "I felt his malevolence, the very evil inside him. He likes it. You said it yourself, he gets off on the terror he creates. He was responsible for those deaths, not you. Surely somewhere in that hard head of yours you know I'm right."

Although he'd heard those very words from his supervisors and coworkers before he'd left his job, he hadn't believed them, at least not then when it had all been so fresh, so terrible. But, now the words coming from her found the wound in his soul and somehow eased a bit of the pain.

"They haunt me, you know," he confessed. "The women he killed. I see them in my dreams."

Her eyes were shiny with emotion and he knew it was for him. She placed a hand on his arm, her fingers warm through the thin fabric of his cotton shirt. He welcomed her warmth, wanted to pull her against him and lose himself in her heat.

"Jacob, you have to play his game again. You have to forget about those other women and focus on the ones who are hopefully still alive."

Her touch no longer felt welcome, but rather burned him. He jerked away from her and stepped back, but she came forward as if refusing to acknowledge his retreat.

"Jacob, for God's sake, he has your sister," she exclaimed. "If for no other reason you have to be involved in this for her."

The words pierced through the veil of denial he'd

tried to erect. Brittany. His heart cried her name and for a moment he felt too weak to stand.

Layla stepped forward and wrapped her arms around his shoulders and pulled herself tight against him. He grabbed on to her as if she were an anchor in a storm-tossed sea.

He felt her heartbeat racing as fast as his own and remembered that she was a part of this, that she had nearly been The Professional's victim.

She trembled in his arms and he tightened his grip on her. She raised her head and looked at him and in her eyes he saw his own emotions mirrored there.

"I'm going to play," he said, knowing he really had no other choice. "I'm going to play his game and hope that this time I find them in time."

Somehow in the depths of his soul he'd known from the moment he'd received the note that he would once again be chasing The Professional and hoping that this time had a different ending.

"I'm afraid, Jacob," she whispered softly.

He once again tightened his grip on her. "It's going to be all right," he replied. He didn't have the heart to tell her that he was absolutely, positively terrified of what was to come.

Chapter 5

Layla awoke to the sounds of men's voices coming from the living room. She assumed Tom and Jacob were having a meeting. She rolled over and grabbed her wristwatch from the nightstand and saw that it was just after eight.

Too early to get up and she didn't want to intrude on the crime-fighting talk going on. She definitely didn't want to know any more details about The Professional and his crimes. She knew all she needed to know about the horror of what he had done, promised yet to do.

Her heart ached as she thought about Jacob. Now they all knew the terrible events that had brought him home, the trauma that had left him with haunted eyes and a scarred heart.

After Tom had left the night before and as she and Jacob had embraced, she'd been afraid for herself, but she'd also been afraid for him. She knew if he was forced to play the madman's game again and things went badly and his sister was murdered, he'd probably never recover from the guilt and grief.

And for a moment, as she'd stood in his embrace, she'd felt connected to him in mind and soul like she had never felt connected to another man. Bound by fear and circumstance to each other, not exactly a good basis for a relationship, she reminded herself.

"Not that I'm looking for a relationship," she muttered aloud.

It wasn't long after that embrace that Jacob had insisted she go to bed. She'd done that, but it had been a long time before sleep had finally found her.

She must have fallen back asleep for when she opened her eyes again it was just after nine and the cabin was silent. Outside the wind whistled, promising a frigid, blustery day. The sunlight was muted, as if its shine was bothered by low-hanging clouds. Maybe the winter storm that had been forecasted for next week was coming in faster than expected.

She got out of bed and pulled her robe on, then left the bedroom to find Jacob standing at the front window, a cup of coffee in his hand. Even though she didn't think she'd made a sound he turned to face her as if he'd sensed her presence.

"I'm going into town around eleven to meet with

Tom and go over his case files on the missing women," he said.

"Then I'm coming with you," she replied. "I can make arrangements to meet Portia or one of my other friends for lunch."

"I don't think that's a good idea," he replied. He looked cold, distant, very different from the emotional, vulnerable man of the night before.

"It's a perfectly fine idea," she countered. "I can ride with you to the sheriff's office and then go to the café for lunch. I'll be surrounded by people and I'm sure I'll be perfectly safe." She didn't want to stay here all alone. "Jacob, we can't be sure that he doesn't know you're here at the cabin. I don't want to be left here without you."

A muscle knotted in his jaw. "You could stay with Edie at the big house," he countered.

She shook her head. "I want to eat lunch out and I'll be just fine."

He frowned. "Okay, you're coming with me but if you can't find a lunch date then you'll have to cool your heels in Tom's office. I don't want you wandering the streets all alone."

"Trust me, I'll find somebody to have lunch with me," she replied and headed for the phone in the kitchen. Portia was thrilled to hear from her and immediately agreed to meet her for lunch.

When it was finally time to leave, Layla couldn't wait to get out of the cabin. Jacob had retreated so far into himself she couldn't reach him. He remained at the window…watching…waiting, an air of expectation keeping his shoulders rigid and his back straight.

Whatever tenuous connection they'd made the night before was gone, swallowed by the darkness of his eyes. She had a feeling he didn't like the fact that she'd seen him vulnerable, that she'd momentarily been his comfort.

A man like Jacob wouldn't tolerate pity and would hate to be seen as weak. She hadn't thought him weak, rather she thought his inner torment spoke of a good man's battle against evil.

At a quarter to eleven they were in his truck and headed into town. "I think it's going to snow," she said as she held her hands out to the warmth of the heater.

"Feels like it," he replied.

"I always hated winter. It's so quiet when the snow falls and my dad didn't work much when it snowed." She turned and looked at Jacob. "He was a construction worker so winter meant he was home most of the time."

"And you didn't like having him home?"

"Not much. He wasn't a very nice man, but that's a whole different story. I hate winter but I love Christmas." She frowned. "And I'm missing the fun of putting up my tree and decorating it. At least it will be fun to have some girl time with Portia."

"Just make sure you stay with her and then come straight back to Tom's office. I don't want anything to happen to you."

"Keep talking like that and I might think you care about me," she said teasingly.

"Strictly business," he replied curtly. "Tom is holding a news conference at noon to remind women to check their backseats before they get into their vehicles and to not wander off alone. He's going to announce that the women of the town shouldn't trust anyone."

"That will stir things up," she replied.

"At this point it's necessary for him to repeat the warnings. Now that we know what we're up against it's important that every woman watch their backs."

"Most of us were already doing that with the disappearances," Layla replied.

"And yet he almost got to you in your car," Jacob countered.

"I got careless," she replied. She frowned thoughtfully. "Tom said that he thought all the women had been taken from their cars. I know Suzy and Jennifer's cars were left at their workplaces and Casey's was still parked in her driveway, but Brittany's was hidden in an old barn."

"Tom and I talked about that this morning. We think maybe he hid her car because he wasn't ready for anyone to know what was going on yet."

"He's smart, isn't he?" She watched as Jacob's features tightened.

"Like a fox."

"Did the FBI ever get close to catching him?"

He hesitated a long moment. "No. We never got close. He was like a ghost in the shadows, a phantom that gave us just enough information to whet our appetites, but he didn't make any mistakes."

Chilling. The whole thing was chilling.

The rest of the ride was accomplished in silence. Layla stared out the window and tried not to think about the killer who was working in their town. Instead she thought about how nice it had felt both times that she'd found herself in Jacob's embrace.

After her nightmare his arms around her had made her feel safe, and last night there had been an intimacy between them that had felt right despite the horrible circumstances.

She glanced at him now and was struck again by the fact that he looked so self-contained, like a man comfortable in his utter aloneness.

He'd told her he didn't do relationships and she wondered what had brought him to that decision. Certainly at the moment he appeared to be a man who needed nobody, but had it always been that way?

By the time they reached the sheriff's office Portia was already there waiting for her. After saying hello to Tom and Sam McCain, one of the other deputies, Layla and Portia left to walk the short distance to the café.

"I've been worried sick about you," Portia said as she leaned into the wind and pulled her collar up closer around her face.

"I'm fine," Layla replied, the wind nearly carrying her words away. "We'll talk when we get inside."

There were few people walking the streets and when

they reached the café they found that many of the usual lunch crowd had apparently opted to spend the bitterly cold day in the warmth of their homes.

They sat at a table near the back and shrugged out of their coats. "Now, how are you really?" Portia asked.

"I'm okay." Layla smiled to assure her friend. "Really."

"When Caleb told me about the attack on you my heart nearly stopped. You must have been so terrified."

"I was," Layla admitted. "But, I feel better staying in the cabin with Jacob. Nothing like having a real live FBI agent at your beck and call."

"I doubt that Jacob is at your beck and call," Portia replied drily. "I can't imagine him doing anything for anyone that he doesn't have to do."

"He's not so bad," Layla said, feeling the need to defend him. "He's had a rough time. Didn't Caleb mention to you what we found out last night?"

"I only saw Caleb for a few minutes this morning and we had some other things to talk about. So tell me what you know."

In a lowered voice Layla told her everything that had transpired the night before. Portia listened wide-eyed as Layla told her about the dead women in Kansas City and The Professional who they now suspected had the missing women from Black Rock.

"That's horrifying," she said when Layla was finished. "It's scary to realize how evil people can be. And it's possible it might be somebody who grew up right here, somebody we all know."

Layla nodded and for the first time looked around at the people inside the café. What would a killer look like? Would he look like Buck Harmon? Buck sat at the counter eating a burger, his long dark hair unruly and his shoulders set in defensive arrogance.

Buck frequented The Edge, a bar on the outskirts of town where Layla occasionally went to dance and have fun. He'd asked her out a couple of times but she'd always turned him down. Buck was trouble and she wanted nothing to do with him.

Or was The Professional an older man? Maybe one of the men seated in a group in the corner? John Mathews, a pleasant-looking man who worked in the bank next to Layla's office, caught her eye and raised a hand in greeting.

The Professional could be anywhere. He could be anyone, somebody they all knew and trusted. He was a monster wearing an ordinary face. Or was it possible he was hiding in the shadows in town? Not somebody they all knew, but rather a drifter who had no real ties to the area?

"Afternoon, ladies. What can I get for you?" Katy Matherson, the waitress, interrupted the direction of Layla's thoughts.

Layla ordered a burger and fries and Portia ordered a salad. Once Katy had departed, Portia leaned back against the red vinyl booth and eyed Layla with concern.

"How are you and Jacob getting along?" she asked.

"I think maybe I'm driving him a little bit crazy," she admitted. "You know me, I like to talk and I don't think he likes to listen to me." She frowned and took a sip of her water. "I think he thinks I'm shallow." She thought of that moment when Jacob had asked her what she had to worry about except the next sale on shoes.

"Then he just doesn't know you very well," Portia replied. She reached across the table and grabbed Layla's hand. "The important thing is that you stay there with him until this crazy man is caught. It doesn't matter what he thinks of you, that's the safest place for you to be right now."

"I know." Layla sighed, her thoughts filled with a vision of Jacob. "I'm attracted to him."

Portia looked at her in dismay. "Oh, Layla, why do you always find yourself attracted to men who are emotionally unavailable?"

"That's not true," Layla protested. "Jackson Michaels wasn't emotionally unavailable." Jackson was the last man she'd dated. The relationship had been hot and heavy for two months and then he'd stopped calling her.

"Then why aren't you still with him?"

Layla frowned thoughtfully. "I don't know. He just stopped calling and that was it." To be perfectly honest, she hadn't been heartbroken. Jackson had been a nice guy, but he hadn't taken her breath away, he hadn't made her wild with desire. He'd just been a comfortable date on lonely nights. "I guess you'd have to ask him why he stopped calling," she finally said.

"Didn't you?" Portia asked.

Layla shook her head. "No, I just figured if he didn't want to see me anymore then that was that."

"Sometimes you have to fight for what you want, Layla. You've dated a lot but you've never fought for any of those relationships to last."

"Life is too short to have to fight for a man. Besides, who needs one? All I said is that I was attracted to Jacob."

The last thing Layla wanted to do was any sort of self-analysis on why she was almost thirty years old and still alone. In her heart she thought maybe her father was right. She was a good-time girl, but not worth a lifetime of love. In any case, she was sorry she'd brought the whole thing up.

"Jacob is damaged goods and that's the last man you need to get involved with," Portia exclaimed.

Thankfully the food arrived and the conversation turned more pleasant. Portia entertained her with stories about her children at the daycare and extolled the virtues of the new assistant she'd hired.

As Portia talked about the kids, Layla found her heart filled with the familiar wistfulness that struck her sometimes when she thought about family. She wanted children. She wanted to be the mother she'd never had to a son or a daughter.

She'd already decided that if she wasn't in a committed relationship by the time she was thirty-five she would either be artificially inseminated or adopt. She wasn't going through her life without knowing the joys of motherhood.

"I've got a secret to share with you," Portia said.

"You know I love secrets," Layla replied. "Spill the beans."

Portia leaned forward, her eyes shining brightly. "I'm pregnant."

Layla stared at her in stunned surprise and then exploded with happiness for her friend. "Oh, my God, that's wonderful news. I know how much you've wanted this."

Portia nodded. "I love taking care of other people's children, but I can't wait to take care of my own."

"I'm assuming you've told Caleb?"

"This morning, that was the only serious conversation we had. He was thrilled, but insists that we need to get married as soon as possible."

"So, you're planning your wedding. How exciting!"

"Nothing big," Portia replied. "Both Caleb and I agree that we're just going to have a quiet, intimate ceremony. Anything else would feel wrong with everything that's going on right now."

Layla felt a whisper of cold breath on her neck as the reality of what had happened once again slammed into her. Four missing women, and she had almost been the fifth.

"I have a huge favor to ask you," Portia said, pulling Layla back from her fear.

"You know I'd do anything for you," Layla replied. She and Portia had been best friends since grade school and it had been Portia's friendship that had gotten Layla through her terrible childhood.

"Be my maid of honor at my wedding."

Layla's heart swelled. "You know I'd love to," she replied. "Now, tell me all the details you're planning for the big day."

They talked about the wedding and were in the middle of talking about Christmas plans when Portia gazed at her wristwatch and frowned.

"I've got to get back to the daycare," Portia exclaimed. "I'm already twenty minutes later than I intended to be. The kids will be wondering about me."

The two women got up and headed to the cashier where they paid for their meals and then stepped out into the cold wind. Portia's car was parked in front of the café but she looped an arm with Layla's. "Come on, I'll walk you back to the sheriff's office."

"Nonsense," Layla exclaimed. "Your car is right here. Get in it and go. Besides, I'm going to stop in my office for just a minute. I left my cell phone there the night of my attack and want to grab it." She untangled her arm from Portia's.

Portia hesitated, a frown tugging across her forehead. "Are you sure? I don't mind going with you."

"You already said you're late. Just go. I'll be fine. It's the middle of the day and I'm sure I can walk a short block without any trouble." She gave Portia a quick hug. "Now get in your car before we both freeze to death."

Before Portia could protest further, Layla started down the sidewalk. The wind seemed to have grown even colder while they'd been eating and she pulled her coat collar up around her neck as she headed toward her office. At least with her cell phone she wouldn't feel so cut off from her normal life.

Two minutes, that's all it would take her to run into her office and grab the phone off her desk. She passed a couple headed toward the café and exchanged a quick smile with them.

The candy cane decorations swung back and forth on the streetlights, buffered by the wind that almost screamed in intensity. They'd be lucky if this cold front and the heavy clouds didn't dump a foot of snow by nightfall.

It wasn't until she dug into her purse for her keys to her office door that the first stir of uneasiness whispered through her. The last time she had left here she'd been attacked. She'd tried to downplay the whole thing at the time that it had happened but now that she had more information about The Professional and the game he liked to play, the horror of how close she'd come to being one of his victims rose up inside her.

Her hand trembled slightly as she shoved the key into the lock. *Get a grip,* she told herself. The danger was past and she'd survived, just as she'd survived every bad moment that had ever happened in her childhood.

She opened the door and stepped inside, immediately spying the blinking light on her answering machine and the jeweled cell phone just where she'd left it.

As she dropped the cell phone into her purse she punched the button to play her messages. "Layla, it's Ginny Sinclair. I was just calling to tell you that I've finally decided to put my mother's house on the market and of course I'd like you to handle it. Call me when you get a chance and we'll meet."

"Yes!" Layla said and pumped her fist in the air. She'd been hoping Ginny would contact her when she was ready to sell. And she already had a couple of buyers in mind.

A second message began to play, the voice a deep, unfamiliar male one. "Yes, my name is Michael Fields and I'm thinking about making Black Rock my permanent home. I'd like to set up a time and place where you could show me some available properties. I'm staying at the Black Rock Motel in unit seven."

He ended the message with his cell phone number, but there was no way Layla intended to plan a tour of properties with any male stranger, not until Mr. Professional was behind bars.

Deciding to make a quick pit stop, she left the main reception area and went down the hallway and into the bathroom. She should tell Jacob and Tom about the caller from the motel. They should check him out to make sure he wasn't dangerous.

When she was finished using the restroom and had washed her hands with the orange-scented soap she loved, she stepped out into the hall and he was there.

She barely had time to process the ski mask that covered his features and the hypodermic needle he held in his hand before he lunged forward to attack.

She screamed and threw her purse at him, adrenaline spiking through her as she turned to run. She'd gone only two steps when he crashed into the back of her.

Her knees smashed to the ground as she fell and she cried out in pain at the same time she tried to scrabble forward like a crab, but he managed to grab her ankle and held tight.

She kicked and screamed again as terror crashed her heart against her ribs. *Get away,* that was the only thought that resounded in her head, obliterating any other thought or sound she might hear.

She had to get away! She didn't want to be a missing person. She refused to go to his party.

Twisting onto her back she managed to break his hold on her ankle. She kicked both legs like motor pistons, gasping in relief as she connected with his hand and the needle flew out of it and skittered along the carpeting to the side of the hallway.

He roared with rage and once again managed to grab

her leg. She twisted and turned in an effort to get free, but his hand was like an iron vise.

Slowly, with deadly intent, he began to pull her along the carpeting toward the needle that she knew meant her death. She knew screaming was useless, that the howl of the wind outside would steal away the sound from anyone who might hear and rush to help.

It was at that moment that Layla knew she was going to die. She was going to be the fifth victim. She'd be the guest of honor at his party. She was going to die because she'd come after her stupid cell phone.

Chapter 6

"We can't assume that he followed me here from Kansas City," Jacob said to his brothers seated around the conference table. "Kansas City is only a three-hour drive from here. It's possible he could be a longtime local and came to Kansas City to commit his crimes."

"That's a scary thought," Benjamin said.

"Were you working with any kind of a profile?" Tom asked Jacob.

"We'd profiled his age to be between thirty and fifty. He's organized with above-average intelligence. He's probably single and is either self-employed or works a job that allows him to work alone for long hours at a time." Jacob leaned back in the hardback chair and frowned as he tried to remember everything they had learned about The Professional, which was damned little.

"You know, the usual stuff, maybe a bed wetter and a fire starter and he probably abused animals at some point in time in his youth," Jacob added. "He's probably narcissistic in personality and suffers from delusions of grandeur, that's evident in the fact that he likes attention."

"Just another garden-variety creep," Tom said with a small smile at Jacob. The smile lasted only a second. "I got a report back early this morning that the drug in the needle found in Layla's car contained a combination of Valium and Versed."

"Versed?" Benjamin looked at him curiously.

Tom nodded. "It's a drug most commonly used for minor health procedures. It would render a person unconscious."

"So, we know our perp either has some medical training or has access to drugs," Jacob replied.

"Nothing any of you have said has narrowed our pool of suspects at all." Frustration was evident in Benjamin's voice.

Jacob looked at Tom. "In all these missing women's cases you didn't find any kind of physical evidence at all?"

"A button," Tom replied. "In Casey Teasdale's car we found a button on the floor of the backseat. It's a slightly oversize white button, but unfortunately there's no way of knowing how long it had been there or if it had anything to do with her disappearance. We tested for fingerprints, but couldn't lift any."

"Right now we don't even have a potential suspect. How are we going to find this guy?" Benjamin exclaimed.

Tom looked at Jacob. "I have a feeling he's going to find Jacob. Didn't you say he communicated with you by phone during the last case?"

Jacob nodded and his cell phone in his shirt pocket suddenly felt as if it weighed a thousand pounds. "To be honest, I'm surprised he hasn't already called me. I never changed my number. I knew he was through with me after the Kansas City debacle."

"Maybe the note that he sent you was just the first contact and the calls will soon start coming," Tom said.

Jacob's stomach turned at the very thought of having to endure another round with the killer. "Maybe this time during the calls he'll make a mistake, give us a clue that we can use to find out his identity. One thing is certain, if he has four women and he's working as he did last time, then he's got them alive and stashed someplace nearby. Maybe an old barn or shed or an abandoned warehouse of some sort."

"We're in the middle of ranch and farming country, almost everyone outside of town has a barn or shed on their property. It's going to be like looking for a needle in a haystack," Benjamin said.

"And Brittany is the needle we're hunting for," Tom

replied, a wealth of emotion in his deep voice. It was the first time any of them had mentioned her name, had acknowledged that she was in the hands of The Professional.

Once again Jacob's stomach churned as he thought of his younger sister. Brittany, with her zest for life and easy sense of humor, had been spoiled by all of her brothers.

They were all different men under their skin, but they all shared a tremendous love for their only sister with her bright green eyes and long dark hair. The idea of her being in the grips of this psychopath made Jacob want to throw up.

As his brother began kicking around ideas and re-hashing the details of the kidnappings, Jacob suddenly thought of Layla and how cold he'd been to her throughout the day.

He'd found comfort in her arms the night before and it had surprised him. He'd thought there was no place in the world he'd ever find comfort again. But Layla's arms had been warm and welcoming and it had scared him more than a little bit.

He didn't want to like her but he did. He didn't want to respect her and yet he did. He definitely didn't want to desire her but he burned with it. What he wouldn't do was allow himself to care about her in any way that involved his heart.

Caleb's cell phone rang. With a quick apology he answered, his face paling as he listened to the caller. "Be right there," he said. "That was Portia. She's at Layla's office and Layla was attacked."

Jacob was out of his chair before the words had fully left Caleb's mouth. As he tore out of the office and into the winter air, a tumble of thoughts went around in his head.

What were they doing in Layla's office? The deal had been she could have lunch with Portia and then return directly to the sheriff's office. Irritation battled with fear as he raced down the sidewalk toward the real estate office.

He was vaguely aware of his brothers' footsteps pounding the pavement just behind him but all he cared about was getting to Layla and making sure she was okay.

He told himself the frantic beating of his heart had nothing to do with his feelings for her, but rather because he felt responsible for her safety.

When he reached her office he slammed through the front door and found the two women in the hallway. Layla lay on her side, curled into a fetal ball and Portia knelt beside her, her pretty face pale with fear.

"He went out the back door," Portia said as she rose to her feet and stepped back against the wall to get out of the way.

As Jacob knelt next to Layla his brothers ran past them to the back of the building. They could deal with the attacker; Jacob's main concern was the woman who looked like a broken doll against the thick beige carpeting.

"Layla, are you all right?" he asked. She nodded her head. Her eyes were closed but silent tears trekked down her cheeks. "Can you sit up?"

He breathed a sigh of relief as she opened her eyes and pulled herself to an upright position. "What happened?"

"I thought I'd just run in and grab my cell phone. I left it here the night I was attacked. No big deal, right?" The words came haltingly from her. "I came in and got the phone off my desk and then decided to use the bathroom. When I came out he was here in the hallway waiting for me."

"Who was here?" Jacob asked even though he suspected what her answer would be.

She shook her head. "I don't know. He had on a ski mask and he had a needle in his hand. I threw my purse at him and tried to run, but he grabbed me from behind. I kicked him and I thought I was going to die. I thought for sure I was going to be another missing woman, and then Portia came in."

She'd begun to tremble, first her lush lips, then her slender shoulders and finally her entire body. It was the tremor of terror.

"I knew she was coming in to get her cell phone and I got in my car and waited for it to warm up before I left. By the time the engine was warm she still hadn't come out," Portia explained. "I don't know why, but I got worried and decided to come in and check on her."

"Thank God you did," Layla exclaimed. She looked up at Jacob, her eyes the color of midnight and haunted. "He wants me to be his number five. I thought maybe he'd just go after somebody else, but he came after me again. He must have been watching me...stalking me." Her voice rose higher and higher in pitch.

Jacob yanked her up to her feet and wrapped an arm around her shoulders, afraid that she was about to get hysterical or go into some sort of shock.

She leaned against him and buried her face into his chest as the tremors continued to suffuse her body. At that moment Tom came back up the hall from the back door.

"Whoever it was, there's no sign of him now." Tom swiped a hand through his dark hair. "The back door lock is broken. We'll need to get a locksmith over here to fix it."

"I'll take care of it," Benjamin said from behind Tom.

Caleb shoved past the two men to get to Portia. When he reached her he pulled her into an embrace. "You could have been hurt," he exclaimed, emotion husky in his voice.

"I'm okay," Portia assured him. "I was never in any real danger. He was already gone by the time I got back here to Layla."

Layla straightened her back and stepped away from

Jacob. "This was all my fault. I was foolish to come in here alone. I'm sorry," she said to Tom. "I'm so sorry," she said to Portia as tears once again began to course down her face.

"Take her back to the cabin," Tom said to Jacob. "We'll take care of things here and I'll come out later to talk to her."

Jacob nodded and once again placed an arm around her shoulders and led her toward the front door. He didn't know whether to be angry with her or feel sorry for her, but one thing was certain, he was afraid for her.

Everything had conspired to make it easy for The Professional to make a move to take Layla. The inclement weather had people staying off the streets, so there had probably been no witnesses. Even if anyone had seen a man in a ski mask they probably wouldn't pay attention to him with the wind howling so bitterly.

He'd apparently jimmied the door lock in anticipation of her eventual return to the office and Layla had presented to him a perfect opportunity by coming in here all alone.

That meant she was right. He'd been watching her... stalking her. She was also correct in her assessment that he wanted to make her, in particular, his fifth victim.

Jacob's heart felt like stone in his chest as he realized it was up to him to keep that from happening. It was up to him to make sure The Professional was caught before he had his party—with Layla as the guest of honor.

* * *

Jacob was quiet on the drive back to the cabin and Layla was grateful. For the first time in her life she didn't feel like talking.

She found herself in a familiar dark place, like the one she'd often found herself in throughout her childhood. It was a place of danger, of uncertainty, and all she wanted to do was find a safe hiding place where nothing and nobody could hurt her.

She'd managed to process the first attack on her. She'd been at the wrong place at the wrong time, a convenient victim he'd thought would be easy to take. She'd been out after dark alone and had probably left her car door unlocked. She'd made herself an easy victim.

But this second attack spoke of something darker. He had to have been watching her, waiting for her to return to her office. He didn't want another woman. He'd chosen her and he wouldn't be happy until he got to her.

"Are you okay?" Jacob finally asked.

"Not really," she replied truthfully. "I'm trying to go to a good place in my mind, but I'm having trouble finding that place."

He flashed her a glance that let her know he had no idea what she was talking about. "Whenever I'm stressed or scared I make a picture in my mind of doing something I like to do," she said in explanation.

"Like buying new shoes."

She nodded. "Something like that. I might imagine myself in a store, or at Portia's daycare with the kids.

When I was younger my favorite place to go in my mind was to imagine I was with my mother. We'd have lunch together or she'd sing to me, you know, I think about the things that make me feel safe and happy."

She looked out the window in time to see them passing the entrance to the Grayson ranch. "Where are we going?"

"I'm going to go to the cabin by some back roads that lead to the property," he replied with a glance in his rearview mirror. "I want to make sure we aren't being followed."

A new chill filled her at this thought. Would he find them at the cabin? Had their security there been breached? "Who is he? How did he know I'd stop in the office today?"

"My guess is that he saw you leave the café and he followed you. Did you see anyone who seemed to be paying particular attention to you in the café or out on the streets?"

"Not really. John Mathews waved at me when I first arrived in the café and Buck Harmon was sitting at the counter. Buck has asked me out a couple of times but I've never gone out with him. You think this might be personal?"

Once again he glanced in the rearview mirror, but apparently saw nothing that alarmed him. "I think all of the women were random victims, chosen only because he knew their routines and knew he could get into the back of their cars. That's one thing that's going to make it more difficult to find him, the fact that the victims were random, and talking to friends and family isn't going to help further the investigation."

"I had certainly become a creature of habit," she said thoughtfully. "Most nights I stayed late at the office and I wasn't always good about locking my car." An edge of anger swept through her. "I made it so easy for him."

"I don't think it started personal with you, but we both know it has become personal." His dark eyes found her again. "There's already been two attempts on you. We don't want a third. We might not get so lucky next time."

Layla leaned forward to adjust the heater vent as his words caused a new chill to race through her. "Do you have nice places you go in your head when you're stressed or upset?" she asked, wanting something to take her mind off the attack.

"I usually go to wherever the bottom of a bottle of beer will take me, but it's usually not a nice place. It's always filled with darkness." His hands tightened around the steering wheel and she knew he was regretting giving her just that much personal information.

Silence reigned for the rest of the drive and finally after twists and turns down back roads they arrived at the shed where Jacob kept his truck. He parked in the shed and they walked the short distance to the cabin.

Overwhelmed. That's what Layla felt as she shrugged out of her coat, sank down on the sofa and watched as Jacob placed a log on the fire and stirred the embers with a poker. He messed in the fireplace until he had flames dancing then he took off his coat and sat in his recliner.

"You want to talk about it?" he asked.

"There's a first, you're inviting me to talk?" She released a deep sigh. "There isn't much to say. I pretty much already told you what happened."

"Did you get any sense of his height? His weight?"

She frowned thoughtfully, remembering that single moment when she'd left the bathroom and had been confronted by the man. "He wasn't as tall as you. I'd say average height and weight. He had on black pants and a brown coat."

"That's good, that's the kind of things we need," he said with encouragement. "Anything else you can think of? Did he talk to you?"

"No, he never said a word. Maybe he was afraid I'd recognize his voice."

"Maybe. Tom is going to be here in a little while. He's going to bring me copies of the case files of all the missing women and he'll want to question you again. Maybe you should make a list of all the men you noticed in the café."

"I can do that," she agreed. "Although I didn't really pay attention to everyone who was there." She opened her purse and pulled out a pen and a diary-size notebook. "I carry this with me and jot down notes about my days," she explained.

She'd always done a little journaling, had started it

when she'd been in fifth grade. It had been a safe way to vent emotions she couldn't speak of out loud. She stared down at the paper and realized her body was beginning to ache from the attack.

"I think before I do this I want to go take a hot shower," she said. "Now that I've started to calm down I'm feeling some bumps and bruises."

Jacob's eyes darkened. "I'll kill him if I get the chance."

The words spoken so calmly, so filled with certainty, shot a mini-chill through her as she got up from the sofa.

Minutes later as she stood beneath the hot spray of water, she understood the darkness that had become Jacob Grayson. The experiences with The Professional had damaged him and there was no way of knowing if that damage could ever be healed.

And now she was wrestling with her own darkness. What worried her more than anything was that since the attack she hadn't found that safe place in her head. The fear from the attack still had her in its grips and no scenario she came up with in her head could take it away.

As a child the mental form of escape had been what made her strong, what had allowed her to endure. Now without that coping mechanism she felt lost.

When this was all over how damaged would she be? Would she ever feel safe again?

By the time she'd finished her shower Tom had arrived

and another round of questions ensued. She could tell him no more than she'd told Jacob although Tom pressed her hard for any impressions she might have gotten from the man who'd attacked her.

She made the list they wanted of everyone she could think of who had been in the café, but there was little more she could do to help with the investigation.

"It's possible you didn't even see him before the attack," Tom said. "He could have come from any of the buildings near your office and sneaked right into the back alley. I've got a couple of men questioning the business owners in the area to see if they saw anything or if anyone suddenly went missing from their work."

"If he can't get to Layla eventually he'll take somebody else," Jacob said. "Eventually his need will drive him to act again."

"All the women in town are on notice, there isn't much else we can do," Tom replied.

He left as dusk was falling and Layla went into the kitchen to cook something for dinner. As she was putting together a meatloaf, Jacob came into the kitchen and sat in one of the chairs at the table.

"It's not your responsibility to cook for me," he said. "I'm sure you probably don't feel like it, especially after the day you've had."

"I like cooking," she replied. "I learned early in life to be good at it." She finished forming the loaf in the pan and then put it in the awaiting oven. "It will take about an hour for that to cook. You want mashed potatoes? Or

I can do scalloped potatoes. Some people like them cut up in wedges and cooked with the meatloaf, but I'm not a big fan of that. Or I could just scrub a couple and put them in the oven to bake." She paused, aware that she'd been rambling. "You really don't care about potatoes, do you?"

"Not really."

She sat opposite him at the table. "I don't know if you've noticed or not but when I'm stressed or upset I tend to talk too much."

"I've noticed." His lips curled up slightly.

For just a moment she thought she saw a faint twinkle in his eyes, like the ghost of the man he'd once been shining through. Her heart did a crazy flip-flop and she wished she'd spent more time with him before The Professional had stolen his soul, wished she'd met him before so much damage had been done.

The twinkle disappeared and the distance she'd come to expect returned as he got up from the table. "Just let me know when it's time to eat," he replied.

Dinner was a silent affair with Jacob not engaging her in any way. When the meal was over and the kitchen was clean, Layla decided to call it a night. It was still relatively early but she was beyond exhaustion and only hoped that she would sleep without dreams.

"I'm going to bed," she said to Jacob, who was once again in his recliner.

"Good night." He remained distant, not taking his eyes off the television screen that played an old movie.

She'd thought that sleep would come quickly due to her exhaustion; however, once she was alone in the bedroom sleep refused to come at all. She twisted and turned, playing and replaying the attack in her mind.

Who was he? Who was this man who called himself The Professional and what was broken inside him that allowed him to do such heinous things?

He'd been so strong as he'd dragged her across the carpeting. If he'd managed to get to that needle and inject her, she now knew she would have gone unconscious. Then it would have been easy for him to carry her out of the building and take her wherever he was holding the other women.

She pulled the quilt up closer around her neck as a shiver worked through her. Twice she'd nearly been a guest at one of his parties. Jacob was right, she might not be so lucky the next time.

What she wanted was somebody to hold her, somebody to tell her everything was going to be all right, but there was nobody. Jacob certainly wasn't up for the task. She wished she at least had Mr. Whiskers with her. He might just be a cat, but he was warm and furry and liked curling up with her during the night. She made a mental note to call Larry Norwood and check how Mr. Whiskers was doing without her.

Mr. Whiskers had been the only male she'd ever been able to count on to love her unconditionally. In her past she had only a father who had abused and belittled her;

in her future she had the potential of becoming a victim of a serial killer. In her present she was completely and utterly alone.

Chapter 7

Jacob sat at the kitchen table, the case files of the missing women spread out before him. He'd contacted his superior at the Kansas City FBI field office to see if he could get any information they might have found on The Professional's crimes since Jacob had left the department. He'd also wanted to find out if there had been any similar crimes committed anywhere else in the country.

His boss had confessed that there had been no further leads on the case and had told Jacob that if Tom wanted FBI assistance in Black Rock all he had to do was request it.

Jacob knew his brother Tom was a prideful man, but that he wasn't so proud he wouldn't ask for help if he needed it. The truth was if The Professional was one of Black Rock's own as they suspected, then the brothers of the Black Rock law enforcement were the best men to find the criminal.

There were no records of similar crimes that had taken place anywhere in the country. It was as if The Professional had come into the age of his reign of terror in Kansas City and now was continuing in Black Rock. Jacob knew that if he was successful here, then it wouldn't be long before another place would soon suffer the same kind of attack.

Criminals like The Professional didn't suddenly stop unless they were placed behind bars or dead. The dark desires that drove him wouldn't be sated for long after one of his parties. He'd soon need another…and another. He had to be stopped here and now.

Was he from Black Rock or had he followed Jacob here? That was the million-dollar question. If they could just pinpoint where The Professional was from they might have a better chance of figuring out who he was.

Jacob leaned back in the chair and glanced at the clock on the wall. Almost midnight. He'd been poring over these files for hours, ever since Layla had gone to bed.

He was looking for something, anything that his brothers and the other deputies might have missed, but so far he'd been unsuccessful in finding anything that might point a finger to any one person in Black Rock, or anywhere else.

He'd asked Tom to come up with a list of people who had recently moved to the area, on the chance that The Professional had followed him from Kansas City to his hometown. He also wanted background searches done on all the doctors in the area and any other hospital personnel who might have access to drugs. An average Joe wouldn't have access to the kind of drugs that had been in the hypodermic needle they'd found in Layla's car.

His brother was returning the next day and hopefully would have a list of names they could begin investigating. It wasn't much to go on, but they had to start somewhere. To keep Layla safe.

Layla.

He got up out of his chair and poured himself a fresh cup of coffee, then returned to the table. Something about Layla was bringing him back to life and he wasn't sure he liked it.

She was making him feel, and he'd believed himself incapable of ever feeling anything again. When he'd seen her curled up on the floor in her office, his heart had nearly burst out of his chest with fear for her.

He didn't want to care about anyone ever again, but Layla had made a chink in his armor, a chink that made him wary. Hell, he was even beginning to find her incessant chatter oddly endearing.

He looked up and nearly jumped in surprise as he

saw the object of his thoughts standing in the doorway wearing that sexy nightgown and matching robe. Her hair was tousled around her face and only made her look sexier than ever.

"Can't sleep?" he asked as a knot of tension wound tight in his stomach.

"No." She walked barefoot to the coffeemaker and poured herself a cup, then grabbed the chair opposite him at the table. She took a sip of the coffee and then lowered the mug from her lips. "I've been tossing and turning and finally decided to give up the battle." She looked at the paperwork in front of him. "Are those the case files of the missing women?"

"Yeah." He stared down at the file in front of him, finding it less provocative than looking at her. "Unfortunately, I haven't been able to find anything that might move the investigation forward in any way."

"So, really the only thing you all have to go on is the drug angle from the syringe that he left in my car."

"That and a button that might or might not have been left by the perp."

"A button?" she asked curiously.

He finally looked at her once again and tried to keep his gaze on her face, not allowing it to drift south. "A white button to be exact." He opened one of the file folders. "There's a picture of it someplace in here. Ah, here it is."

He slid the picture across the table toward her. She picked it up and studied it. "Too big to be a shirt button," she observed. "Looks more like a coat or some sort of decorative button. Where was it found?"

"In Casey Teasdale's car. Did you know her?"

She nodded and slid the photo back to him. "Casually. She was a trendy dresser. It's possible the button came off a dress or a jacket of hers."

"Did you know my sister?" He wasn't sure why he'd asked or why it was important to him. For the first time since this all had begun he wanted, needed, to talk about his sister.

"I know Brittany," she replied, making him realize he'd spoken of his sister in the past tense. "We're friendly, but don't really hang out together. She's a beautiful woman, Jacob, and I know you and your brothers are going to do everything in your power to bring her home."

Emotion pressed thick and tight in his chest. He'd tried not to think about his sister at the hands of The Professional, but now thoughts of Brittany filled his head, his heart. Would she be home for Christmas? Or would they find her body after The Professional had enjoyed his party?

"She's tough," he finally said.

"Tell me about her," Layla urged him, as if sensing his need to talk about her.

"She's sometimes irresponsible, which is why my brothers didn't realize she was initially missing. It wasn't until she'd missed a couple of days of work that we realized there was a problem. Still, she'd missed work before and Caleb, Benjamin and Tom had always covered for her. We all spoiled her terribly over the years."

"I imagine having four big brothers isn't the easiest thing in the world at times," Layla replied.

An unexpected laugh blurted out of him. "She used to complain that it was like having four overly protective fathers." He leaned back in his chair. "She loves to sing and is completely tone-deaf, but she has a heart of gold and would do anything for anyone." Any laughter he might have felt faded away beneath a crushing weight of anguish. "She's got to be all right."

"She's still alive, Jacob. Hang on to that," Layla said softly. "He hasn't had his final party yet, and as long as he doesn't there's still a chance for Brittany and all the other women."

He nodded. "If anyone can survive this ordeal, she can. We just need to find them before he snaps again."

"Or before he gets me." Layla's voice held a slight tremor that spoke of her own fear. "I don't want to be a guest at his party."

"We're not going to let him get to you," he said, a rough edge to his voice.

"Promise?"

He sighed. "The last time I made a promise I made it to Carrie Walker's mother. I promised her I'd find her daughter before The Professional killed her, but Carrie was one of the women we found in that warehouse. I don't make promises anymore, not about anything."

"Well, I can promise you that I don't intend to go

into my office alone again until this is all over." She wrapped her fingers around her mug and brought it to her lips. He couldn't help but notice that her hands trembled slightly.

"I'm sorry you're frightened," he said.

She lowered her cup and offered him a small smile. "Thanks. I'll be fine. This isn't the first time in my life I've been afraid. True fear is being eight years old and hiding under a porch. Real terror is knowing that if your father finds you it might be the time he finally beats you to death."

Jacob stared at her in stunned surprise. "Your father was abusive?"

She set her cup on the table and her eyes were dark with memories he could only guess were terrible. "My father was a brutal bastard. The only good thing he did for me was die. Surprisingly, he had a very big life insurance policy on himself and left me as beneficiary. And you probably think I'm terrible for saying that."

"I don't think you're terrible at all." He'd sensed that there was more to Layla West than her chattiness and superficial values. He realized now there had been clues about her father, he just hadn't picked up on them. "You never tried to get help from anyone?"

Again she smiled, a small gesture that didn't quite lighten the darkness of her eyes. "For a long time I just assumed everyone's dad was mean. By the time I knew that something was wrong I was too scared of him to tell anyone. The day I turned eighteen I left his house and got myself an apartment. Between then and the time of his death we didn't have a relationship at all."

"It was his loss," Jacob replied.

This time her eyes lit up. "Thanks. Anyway, I figure I survived him. I can survive this." There was a hint of steely strength in her voice. "And that's why I like shoes," she added.

Jacob frowned in confusion. "What do shoes have to do with all this?" Sometimes the way her mind worked fascinated him.

"Shoes are my rebellion against the man who raised me. Every year at Christmas he bought me a pair of shoes, the ugliest sturdy brown shoes you'd ever want to see. I hated those damned shoes. Kid at school made fun of them. I decided when I got old enough to buy my own, I'd make sure they were pretty, sexy high heels and I'd have a different pair for every day of the year."

"You don't owe me any explanation for what you buy," he protested.

"I know, but I suspect you think I'm kind of shallow and I just wanted you to know that there is a method to my madness. I paid my penance for future sins by enduring my father and now I just want to live life to its fullest. By the way, I think you've more than done your penance for a sin you didn't even commit." She leaned forward, her eyes ablaze with emotion. "Just catch this man, Jacob, and in the process give yourself permission to live again."

He wanted her now, with her eyes so bright and the

sweet words of redemption on her lips. He wanted to carry her into the bedroom and take her until they were both left gasping and spent.

But he knew he wasn't going to do that. He had nothing to give her except his momentary passion, his quick-fire desire, and it didn't seem fair to offer her that and nothing else.

"Why aren't you married, Layla?"

She shrugged her shoulders. "I'm just not the marrying kind," she replied.

"So, you have no desire to have a family?"

"On the contrary, I definitely want kids," she replied. "I figure by the time I'm thirty-five if I haven't found a man who'd be a good father, then I'll just get artificially inseminated and have my baby. I don't need a man in my life to be a good mother."

He wondered how deep the scars were from her childhood with her father. Was his brutality why she wasn't the marrying kind, why she didn't think a father was important in the life of a child?

"There are men out there who would make great fathers," he said.

"I suppose. And on that note, I think maybe it's time for me to try to get some sleep." She stood and carried her cup to the sink.

"Yeah, I need to do the same," he agreed. He closed the case files and stacked them, then got up and took his cup to the sink. He turned to tell her good-night and found her standing far too close to him.

The flowery, feminine scent of her filled the air and the desire he'd tamped down only moments before roared to life once again.

"Then I guess I'll just say good night," she said. She licked her lower lip and Jacob knew in that instant that he was going to kiss her.

She must have sensed it as well, for she made no move to back away from him or go to her bedroom. Instead she leaned forward at the same time he took a small step to close the short distance between them.

The instant his mouth touched hers, he knew he was in trouble. Hot and greedy, her lips instantly yielded to his, opening enough to allow him to deepen the kiss.

At the same time her arms went up to his shoulders and he found himself gathering her close, the slick material of the silk robe warming as his hands splayed across her slender back.

The kiss spiraled out of control quickly. He tangled his hands in her soft, scented hair as their tongues swirled in a fevered dance.

Her robe gaped open as she pressed even closer to him, so close he could feel the fullness of her breasts against him, felt the hard pebbles of her erect nipples through the thin material of her nightgown.

She was fire and vibrant energy in his arms and he wanted to take whatever she offered, whatever he needed from her. He wanted to take until she had no more left to give and then he'd take some more.

For the first time in over six months he felt wonderfully

alive, his mind emptied of all thought except his want of the woman he held in his arms.

He moved his mouth from her lips to her jaw, then down the length of her neck, his heart pounding rapidly in his veins. She dropped her head back, allowing him access to the column of her throat, and as she released a small moan, his desire torched hotter, brighter.

There was no thought of what he couldn't give her, no thought of how wrong this moment was for both of them. There was only her heat, her fire that warmed him in places that had been cold for a very long time.

"Jacob," she whispered, his name a fevered plea for more and more.

And he wanted more. God help him but he wanted all of her. He released his hold on her and stepped back, giving them both a moment to draw in deep breaths, to ground them in reality.

She obviously didn't want reality. She held out her hand to him, her eyes speaking of her own desire, and he knew he was going to take her into her bedroom and stay with her until their desire was sated.

The bedroom was dark when they entered and she dropped his hand only long enough to turn on the bedside lamp. It created a soft pool of illumination that loved the hues of her skin.

She shrugged off her robe and his gaze was drawn to the flush of her cheeks, then the fullness of her breasts beneath the animal print gown.

He'd been numbed by his pain, by his very solitude

for some time. But he didn't feel numb at the moment. Rich and raw desire filled him as he advanced toward her.

"No promises," he said, his voice sounding deeper than usual.

"None needed," she replied easily. "Just give me tonight with you, Jacob. I won't ask you for anything more."

That was all he needed to hear, the acknowledgment that she expected nothing from him except this night and his passion. He took her back into his arms.

At that moment his cell phone rang.

The musical ring sliced through the sexual tension as confusion washed over him. Who would be calling him at midnight?

The confusion swiftly gave way to a fear that instantly washed all his desire away. He dropped his arms from around Layla and stared at her as the phone rang again.

"Don't answer," Layla said urgently as he dug his cell phone out of his pocket. "Please, Jacob. Just don't answer it." It was as if she knew who might be on the other end of the line.

He stared down at the number on his caller identification, not recognizing the digits that were displayed. He opened the phone and placed it against his ear, but said nothing.

"Hello Agent Grayson. I've missed you. Are you ready to play?"

The deep, familiar voice cast Jacob back into the darkness and it was only the touch of Layla's hand that kept him from drowning in it.

Chapter 8

"I couldn't hear anything in the background of the call that might point to a location," Jacob said to his brothers, who were all squeezed around the cabin's small kitchen table. Outside the day was as dismal and gray as the mood among the men.

"We've gone over this a dozen times already," he said impatiently. "I didn't recognize his voice, it was distorted as it's always been. All he said was that he's looking forward to playing the game with me, that Jennifer Hightower cries all the time and Suzy Bakersfield appears to be in a mild state of shock. And Brittany said to tell me hello."

As the men continued their discussion Layla silently refilled their coffee cups. She'd gotten up early that morning and fixed Jacob breakfast. He'd said he wasn't hungry, but she'd insisted he eat, knowing that it was going to be a long day.

The night before had seemed endless. After the phone call, Jacob had insisted she go to bed, and sensing he wanted time alone, she'd complied. She'd found sleep impossible and knew he'd suffered the same fate as she'd heard him wandering around the cabin until nearly dawn.

She hadn't been sure if it was the phone call or the fact that they'd almost made love that had kept sleep at bay for her. The contact with the killer had been disturbing, but so had the intimate contact with Jacob.

Jacob moved her as no other man in her life had ever done before.

She would have fallen into bed with him last night if the phone call hadn't interrupted them. And he would have taken her to bed. He'd kissed her with raw desire. There had been no mistaking what he wanted from her.

And she'd wanted him like she'd never wanted before. She would have willingly capitulated to her own wants, her own needs, if that horrifying call hadn't happened.

She tucked a strand of her hair behind her ear and tried not to dwell on the thoughts of what might have been, but they kept intruding into her brain.

She knew better than to chase what she couldn't have, and Jacob was in that category. Oh, she might get his passion, enjoy his lust, but she knew there would never be anything deeper, more lasting.

Sometimes she felt as if her father had cursed her just to be spiteful. He'd made a deal with the devil to keep her from finding real love.

Jacob looked both tired and slightly dangerous in his black turtleneck and jeans and wearing his shoulder holster. He'd had the gun on when she'd gotten up that morning, the result of the contact with the killer and a reminder that danger could come at any time.

She finished pouring their coffee and then resumed her stance in the corner, her gaze lingering on Jacob. The lack of sleep the night before showed in tired lines that bracketed his mouth, in the faint shadows beneath his eyes.

What she'd like to do was pull him into her bed, force him to sleep without dreams and sleep wonderfully well-embraced in his arms. She closed her eyes and for a moment imagined herself there, in the safety and security of his strong arms.

"Okay. So we didn't get anything from the phone call. I've got a couple of the men searching all the abandoned buildings here in town," Tom said as Layla tried to focus less on Jacob and more on the conversation. "And when we're finished in town we'll spread out and begin checking buildings around the area."

"That's going to be a huge job," Benjamin observed.

"I agree," Tom replied. "I've called up all the volunteer deputies to come in and help with the search and the men from the fire department have also offered to step in and do whatever they can to help."

"This is a good town," Benjamin added. "People will step up to stop this lunatic."

"Caleb came up with a list of people who have moved to Black Rock in the last six months or so," Tom continued and looked at his youngest brother.

"There's only been a couple of people," Caleb said as he pulled a piece of paper from his pocket. "Jerry Tipton is thirty-two and moved here four months ago. He's divorced and works as a traveling salesman for some grocery company. Then we have Greg Todd. He's twenty-nine and moved here a couple of months ago and works as a nurse at the hospital. Finally, there's the Norwood family. Larry, his wife and their two daughters moved here about seven months ago."

"I investigated Larry Norwood when Lilly was kidnapped," Tom replied. "He doesn't exactly fit our profile in that he appears happily married and obviously has a love for animals, since he's a veterinarian."

"The profile is sometimes wrong," Jacob replied. "We can't overlook anyone."

There was no way Layla would believe that Larry Norwood could be The Professional. He was caring for her cat, for goodness' sake.

"We'll do full background checks on these people," Tom said. "At least it's a place to start."

"I'd like to talk to all of them," Jacob said. "If one of them is The Professional I might not recognize the voice but I could pick up something in their speech patterns that would identify him."

"I'll arrange interviews with all of them in my office," Tom said.

"As a nurse it's possible that Greg Todd would have access to the kind of drug we found," Benjamin said.

"Anyone can access any drugs on the internet these days," Jacob reminded them.

"A traveling salesman would have opportunity," Caleb added.

"We'll check them out," Tom said. "Once they're cleared with alibis or whatever, we'll move to long time residents of Black Rock that might be responsible."

"Like Buck Harmon?" Layla asked.

Tom leaned back in his chair and smiled at her. "Buck is a pain in my ass, there's no question. He drinks too much and when he drinks he gets stupid, but I'd bet my badge he isn't a killer."

"Buck Harmon isn't organized enough to find his way home on a Saturday night," Benjamin said wryly.

"I just thought of something," Layla said, suddenly remembering the phone message she'd received in her office. "When I was at my office I listened to my messages and there was one from a man. He said his name was Michael Fields and that he was planning on making Black Rock his home. He's staying at the motel and he wanted me to take him out to look at properties."

"Did you contact him while you were there?" Tom asked.

She shook her head. "I wrote down his phone number but I didn't call him back. He's staying in unit seven at the motel. Maybe it's him. Maybe he's The Professional."

She frowned as she thought of what might have happened if she'd taken him out. Would she have shown him an empty house where he could have overwhelmed her and carried her off?

"We'll definitely check it out," Tom replied.

"Maybe it's him, but I'm inclined to think not," Jacob replied. "As far as we could tell in the other cases, he never contacted his victims."

"And there's no evidence that he did so in these current cases," Benjamin added.

"But somebody here in town is a killer," Layla replied. "And he wants me."

"He doesn't like to lose," Jacob said. "And you've thwarted his efforts twice now." His gaze held hers for a long moment and in his eyes she thought she saw a hint of softness. "Is there someplace else you can go?" he asked. "Family or friends or somebody you can stay with until this mess is all over?"

She shook her head. "I don't have any family and all my friends are right here in Black Rock." She raised her chin defensively. "Besides, he's got me staying here in this cabin where no hint of Christmas exists, he's got my cat boarded at the vet's office and me staying away from my office. He's taken enough from me already. I'm not leaving town."

She was suddenly aware of Tom staring at her, his eyes narrowed thoughtfully. "I'm not sure I want you to leave town," he said slowly. "Maybe it's a good idea for you to be seen in town, to let him know that you're still here and aren't afraid. Maybe it will push him to do something stupid."

"Whatever I can do to help, I'll do," Layla replied, ignoring the flutter of fear that winged in her stomach.

"Or it will push him to do something terrible," Jacob said darkly.

Layla wanted to place her hand on his shoulder as she saw the shadows that had crept back into his eyes. She knew he was remembering when he'd thought he'd been the one who had pushed the killer too far and death had resulted.

"He's going to do something terrible whether we push him or not," Tom replied. "And we'll do whatever is necessary to keep Layla protected."

As the men continued to discuss their plans to further the investigation, she remained in her place in the corner, listening to the conversation that eased none of her fears.

It was almost noon when Layla and Jacob were alone again. Jacob was quiet, but it wasn't the morose kind of silence she'd endured the first night and day with him. It felt like a focused silence, as if his head was filled with plans and thoughts that brooked no discussion.

"No more fires," he said when she started to place a log into the fireplace.

She looked at him in surprise. "Why not?"

"We don't want to send up any more smoke signals that will let anybody know that we're here."

His words sent a new sense of disquiet through her as she placed the log back in the wooden box by the fireplace. "Does this mean we'll freeze to death?"

He cast her a tired smile. "No, it just means I need to turn up the thermostat on the furnace." He sank into his recliner with a deep sigh.

"Portia is pregnant," Layla said, suddenly remembering her friend's good news from the day before. She had no idea what made her think of it but suspected it was her mind subconsciously working to stay positive.

Jacob raised an eyebrow. "She is? Caleb hasn't mentioned anything about it, but I guess the circumstances haven't exactly been great for him to make an announcement. He must be thrilled. He always wanted a family."

"Did you ever want children?" she asked.

"I thought about it once, but things didn't work out." He leaned back in the chair and stifled a yawn with the back of his hand. "It was a long time ago and I was a different man then." These words were spoken with an edge of bitterness in his voice that invited no further questions.

"Why don't you take a nap while I make us some lunch," she suggested.

"That sounds like a plan," he agreed. "And for dinner tonight you and I will eat at the café."

"Why do I suddenly feel like a minnow?"

"Layla, you know I won't let anything happen to you, but I think maybe Tom is right. Both of us need to be seen around town. Maybe if we flaunt our presence in his face, he'll get so angry he'll show his hand." His eyes suddenly went black. "Let's just hope we don't push him so hard that those women wind up dead before we catch him."

"That's not going to happen this time, Jacob," she said fervently. She knelt down next to his chair and laid her head on his upper arm. "This is going to have a better ending."

"You promise?" he asked softly, his voice already filled with imminent sleep.

Before she could reply she knew he'd fallen asleep. She rose from his side and watched him for several long moments. His chest rose and fell in a slow, deep rhythm and once again she thought of what it would be like to be held in his arms. She found herself wondering what it would be like to be loved by a man like Jacob.

Irritated with this kind of thought she left him and went into the kitchen to prepare some sort of lunch for them. Within minutes she was engrossed in putting together a quick sauce for spaghetti.

So, there had been a woman, she thought. Things didn't work out, that's what he'd said and that implied there had been a relationship once.

Whoever she was, Layla suspected she had broken his heart. Once again Layla found herself wishing she'd connected with Jacob sooner, before the woman, before The Professional.

She chided herself inwardly. The last thing she wanted to do was develop any real feelings for Jacob. She didn't want to feel that heady rush of emotions, the hope that somehow she'd find her soul mate. She'd been disappointed so many times in the past and didn't want to go through it again.

It was easier to not involve her heart, to go through the motions of a relationship without expecting, without hoping for anything other than a few laughs and a couple of nights. Loving Jacob would be the worst thing she could do.

It took her nearly an hour to get the sauce and spaghetti ready. She made a salad and broiled some bread with a little butter and garlic topping, then set everything on the table.

Satisfied that it was ready to eat, she stepped into the living room and froze. Jacob wasn't in the recliner. Her gaze shot to the bathroom door. It was open and it was easy for her to see that nobody was inside.

Don't panic, she told herself, but when she checked the bedroom and didn't find him there, a sweeping anxiety overtook her. Where had he gone?

On wooden legs she walked to the front door. His coat was no longer hanging on the hook next to hers. She looked outside, but saw no sign of him.

The anxiety blossomed into something stronger. Had he tired of her? Had she pushed him too hard with personal questions, talked too much and driven him crazy?

Or had he somehow gotten a clue who The Professional was and gone after him without the support of his brothers, with only his rage to back him up?

No, she didn't believe he'd done that. She'd sat in on the conversation that had taken place around the kitchen table. There was no way Jacob could have gleaned the identity by that conversation.

It was more likely she'd driven him crazy, with her talk about shoes and children, with her endless nervous chatter about everything under the sun.

She remained at the door, staring outside as a new emotion shoved up in her chest. A weary resignation filled her. She shouldn't be surprised if he'd left for good. Even with the threat of death hanging over her head she couldn't keep a man at her side. It was just like her daddy had always told her.

Jacob made his way through the thick woods near the cabin, wondering what in the hell had possessed him. But he knew. Layla. She had possessed him.

He knew this land as well as he knew the sound of his own breathing. During the last six months of isolation he'd often walked these woods at dusk, thinking about the past and the part he'd played in the deaths of The Professional's first victims.

Somehow over the last couple of days rational thought had sliced through the fog of despair that had settled over him since he'd arrived back in Black Rock.

He no longer carried the weight of those deaths in his heart. Layla had been right when she'd told him that the women were already dead the moment The Professional had taken them. Jacob also suspected The Professional had meant to make Jacob feel responsible when he'd claimed Jacob had pushed him over the edge. The killer was already over the edge and his words to Jacob had just been more of his manipulation and game-playing.

At least there had been no report of any other woman missing. Tom's press conference had put the women of Black Rock on notice. There was a killer among them and care should be taken not to be out alone.

Of course, Jacob still believed that Layla was the chosen fifth victim and The Professional wouldn't be happy with anyone else, but the problem was he wasn't sure. He couldn't anticipate anything when it came to this particular serial killer.

It took him only minutes to find what he was looking for. Using the ax he'd brought with him he cut down the small evergreen tree. He'd also brought with him a bucket perfect to fill with dirt to stand the tree upright.

He had no idea how long he and Layla would be cooped up together in the cabin. It was possible they would be there through the holidays and she was missing the Christmas season, so he'd decided to bring a little of it into the cabin.

With the tree set in the bucket he picked it up and headed back and his heart felt lighter than it had in a very long time. He had no Christmas decorations for the tree, but he had a feeling Layla was creative enough to make a purse out of a sow's ear.

When he reached the porch she flew out of the door, her face pale as she trembled with something that looked very much like anger.

"How could you?" she demanded and slapped her hands against his chest. "How could you just disappear like that and not tell me where you were going?"

"I thought I'd surprise you," he offered, aware that it had been a mistake on his part not to tell her he was going out. He'd been alone too long and it had been thoughtless. "Get inside before you catch cold."

She turned on her high heels and stomped back through the door. Jacob followed her, aware that he owed her an apology. "I'm sorry," he said as he set the tree down next to the fireplace. He shrugged out of his coat and hung it up.

"I just thought you'd left, that maybe I'd driven you away because I talk too much." Her voice trembled slightly.

"I hate to admit this, but I'm getting used to your chatter," he said with a small smile. "You'd mentioned a couple of times that there was no Christmas here, so I thought I'd bring you a little." He sat on the sofa next to her. "Layla, I'm not going to leave you until this is all over, until I know for sure you're in no danger. Again, I apologize for scaring you. And now I smell something delicious so let's eat and then you can figure out how to make this little evergreen tree into a Christmas tree."

She could have held a grudge. God knew Sarah had been able to hold a grudge for hours, even days, over some perceived slight. But, Layla was back to herself as they ate lunch, chattering about the holidays and asking him about favorite Christmas traditions from his youth.

"Aluminum foil stars," she said suddenly. "That's how we can decorate the tree. And popcorn." She jumped out of her chair and went to the pantry. "Got it," she exclaimed triumphantly as she pulled out a box of microwave popcorn. "This will be so much fun," she said as she returned to the table. "We'll spend the afternoon creating a stunning masterpiece."

"Whoa, the tree was a project for you. I've got other things to do this afternoon," he protested.

"Like what?" she demanded. She leaned forward and grabbed his hand across the table. "Let it all go, Jacob. For just a couple of hours let it go and let's have fun."

Fun? He couldn't remember the last time he'd allowed himself that. Staring into her hopeful eyes he realized he wanted a little fun with her. He wanted those couple of hours of not thinking about danger and death, of not allowing The Professional to enter his mind.

"You're going to have to teach me how to make aluminum foil stars," he replied.

She smiled in delight. "I'd be happy to."

Within thirty minutes they had finished the meal, cleaned up the dishes and were seated at the table with a box of aluminum foil while the scent of freshly popped popcorn filled the air.

"Christmas was never any big deal when I was growing up," she said as they worked the foil to create stars. "Once I left my father's house I made it a big deal every year. I usually decorate my house like the North Pole, bows and ribbons and holly everywhere."

"Christmas was a big deal at home when I was a kid," he replied. His head was suddenly filled with the memory of those days when his parents had been alive and all his brothers and his sister were beneath one roof.

He'd loved being part of his family unit and at that time had promised himself that when he got older and married he'd fill his house with children and laughter.

He'd not only done a disservice to himself, but also to the memory of his parents by closing himself off from his family the last six months.

"Mr. Whiskers loves Christmas, too," Layla said, pulling him from his thoughts.

"How long have you had Mr. Whiskers?" he asked.

"Two years. I got him as a kitten because I felt like I needed something living and breathing in my house besides myself. I wanted something to come home to, something to take care of and Mr. Whiskers was my answer."

He nodded, but in her words he sensed a depth of

loneliness that was belied by his perception of Layla West. She was vibrant and beautiful and he couldn't imagine a woman like her ever being lonely.

"Maybe you need a pet," she said and smiled at him. "Have you ever considered getting a dog or a cat, something you could take care of? Something that would love you unconditionally? You know studies say that pets are good for your mood and good for high blood pressure."

He laughed. "What makes you think I might suffer from high blood pressure?"

"I don't see how you wouldn't have high blood pressure considering the job you chose." She set aside the star she'd just finished. "Did you like your work…I mean, before The Professional?"

He stared out the window where a false twilight had fallen despite the fact it was only four o'clock. He felt as if he'd been in the middle of a false twilight for months.

"Yeah, I loved what I did," he finally replied. He got up from the table and walked over to the window where he stared out unseeing. "I felt like I was doing something good, something important. I like law enforcement and I allowed him to take that away from me."

He wasn't aware that she'd left the table until she touched his back. It was a soft touch, meant to comfort. "You could go back, couldn't you?"

He considered her words thoughtfully and then shook

his head. "No, I don't think so. It's been too long and it wouldn't be fair to the other agents who stuck it out."

"Then what are you going to do? You can't stay here, cooped up for the rest of your life."

He turned to face her then. "To be honest I haven't given it much thought. Maybe I'll see if Tom could use another deputy here when this is all over." He smiled then, hoping to take away the concern that darkened her beautiful eyes. "Or maybe I can set up a booth and sell aluminum stars."

She smiled then, just as he suspected she would and the warmth of it sizzled through him, along with the memory of the kiss they'd shared.

He wanted to kiss her again. He knew it would be a mistake, but he didn't care. He had scarcely moved a muscle before she was in his arms, her mouth locked with his in a kiss that took his breath away.

Someplace in the back of his mind he knew this wasn't right, that there was no way he was willing to put his heart on the line again. But another voice reminded him that he'd made that clear to her, that she knew the score and it didn't seem to matter to her.

Take what she gives, the voice said. Don't overthink it, just go with the flow. The flow was in the sweet spill of her hair in his fingers, in the heat of her lips against his.

"Oh, Jacob," she murmured against his mouth. "I want you. Take me into the bedroom and make love to me."

His heart accelerated in rhythm as his body responded

to her nearness, her words. But he had to be certain that she understood. He had to tell her again that she should expect nothing more from him than a physical connection that had no future.

"Layla." He stepped back from her. "If we do this then you have to understand that it's a one-shot deal and there's no future with me."

"I live in the moment, Jacob. Besides, I already told you I'm not the marrying kind." She moved back into his arms, her eyes shining overly bright. "Just give me this moment with you."

How could he deny her what he wanted most? Together they left the kitchen and went into the bedroom. Once there he kissed her again, the kiss quickly growing to a fever pitch.

He knew there were condoms in the bottom drawer of the nightstand. Throughout the last couple of years his brothers had occasionally entertained women in the cabin.

He broke the kiss once again, this time to remove his holster and set it on top of the nightstand. As he did that, Layla pulled her sweater over her head, revealing a black lace bra that nearly had him finished before he'd begun.

Yanking the turtleneck he wore over his head, his heart thundered. It had been so long since he'd enjoyed the pleasures of a woman's body, so long since he'd felt this well of need.

She kicked off her high heels and then peeled off her

jeans, revealing panties that matched the black bra. "You are so beautiful," he said softly.

She smiled and slid beneath the quilt on the bed. "And right now I'm all alone."

He was just about to unfasten his jeans when a bang of metal came from outside. Somebody was out there! Instantly he reached for his gun, all thoughts of lovemaking banished by a different kind of adrenaline.

Layla shot up to a sitting position, her eyes huge with fear. "Jacob?"

"Stay inside. Don't open the door to anyone but me," he said as he ran for the front door. His thoughts zoomed through his head. Who was outside? If it was one of his brothers they would have made themselves known.

Was it possible their hiding place had somehow been found? Was it The Professional outside seeking a way in? Even the reassuring weight of his gun in his hand couldn't take away the chill of imminent danger that worried through him as he opened the door and stepped out into the shadows of pre-dusk.

Chapter 9

The minute Jacob left the bedroom Layla scrambled out of bed and pulled her robe around her. Her heart banged painfully fast against her ribs as she hurried toward the front door and peered outside. There was no sign of Jacob or anyone else.

Had The Professional found them? There was no question in her mind that he would kill Jacob to get to her. Tears blurred her vision as she gripped the door frame on either side.

Jacob! Her heart cried with fear for him. He shouldn't have gone outside. He should have called for backup. He was just starting to live again and it wasn't fair that he might die in his effort to keep her safe.

She should have grabbed her cell phone as she'd run

from the bedroom. She was just about to go retrieve it and call for help when Jacob appeared at the door.

Quickly she unlocked it and threw herself at him. "Oh, thank God," she exclaimed.

"It was a false alarm," he said. "A stray dog was trying to find a meal in my trash can around back." He patted her back. "It's okay, you're safe."

"I wasn't worried about me, I was terrified for you," she confessed as she clung with her arms around his shoulders. She buried her face in his chest, his skin cold from his outing without a shirt. "I was afraid it was him and that he'd kill you."

"Nobody is going to kill me if I can help it," he replied, his voice lower than usual as he tightened his arms around her.

She didn't reply. She wanted to warm him, needed to continue to touch him, to assure herself that he was alive and well.

The moment in the bedroom had been broken by the noise and Jacob's rush outside, but it hadn't taken away her intense desire for him, it hadn't banished her need to belong to him completely, even if there was no happily-ever-after attached.

She finally raised her head and looked at him. "Now, where were we?" She was determined to get what she wanted, and she wanted Jacob.

His eyes flashed with fire that threatened to combust her where she stood. "I remember exactly where we were."

"Then why don't we resume where we left off?" She

stepped out of his arms and turned to go back into the bedroom, confident that he would follow.

Once again he set his gun on the nightstand within easy reach as she shrugged out of her robe and got into the bed. She watched silently as he took off his shoes and socks and then shrugged out of his jeans.

As he stood at the side of the bed clad only in a pair of navy briefs, her breath hitched in her chest. He might think she was beautiful half-clothed, but he was absolutely magnificent.

His torso was long and lean, his shoulders broad and his legs powerful. But it was those eyes of his that captured her, so dark and hungry as they gazed at her.

He slid into the bed next to her and she shivered in sweet anticipation as he drew her into his arms. His body was no longer cold, but rather wonderfully warm.

Their lips met in a kiss that stole her breath and made her utterly boneless in his arms. She suspected she'd wanted him the moment she'd walked into the cabin and saw him, so brooding and broken. But he didn't feel broken now—he was filled with vibrant energy.

He splayed his fingers across the naked skin of her back, his touch hot and welcome. She wanted his hands everywhere, on her back, on her breasts and anywhere else. She felt as if her skin was starved for his very touch.

"I feel like I've wanted you forever," she whispered.

"I feel the same way." His hands found the clasp of her bra and in the blink of her eye she felt it unfasten.

She rolled over and straddled him as she allowed her bra to fall from her shoulders. She closed her eyes as he reached up to caress her bare breasts and then moaned as his thumbs raked across the tips.

She could feel his arousal beneath her and she wanted him on top of her, inside her. She rolled back to the side of him and stripped off her panties, then tugged impatiently at the waistband of his briefs.

"Not so fast," he protested. "Slow, Layla, I want to take it slow."

And he did take it slow. His hands moved with languid but studied intent, as if memorizing the weight of her breasts and the span of her waist. His lips moved slowly, too, drawing in each of her nipples in turn, into his mouth and creating exquisite sensations that shuddered through her.

Magic. He was sheer magic and he made her feel like the most beautiful woman on earth. As he gazed at her with his onyx eyes that sparked with such fevered need, she felt his magic in the very depths of her soul.

When his hand moved down the flat of her belly, a small moan escaped her. And when he touched her as intimately as a man could touch a woman she was instantly at near-orgasm.

As he moved his fingers against her, she cried out his name, stunned by the tidal wave of pleasure that swept over her again and again until she was weak and gasping for breath.

It was then, when she was limp and shuddering in his

arms, that he moved away from her just long enough to take off his briefs.

He fumbled in the nightstand and then she realized he'd grabbed a condom wrapper. "Wait," she said as he tore it open. "I want to touch you before you put it on." She wanted to feel his warm flesh in her hand, feel the pulse of the power inside him.

As she took hold of him he groaned in pleasure and when she stroked her hand up and down the hard length of him he stopped her. "Don't," he said in a voice that sounded half-strangled. "I don't want it to be over this way."

Neither did she so she pulled back her hand as he put on the condom. When it was in place he rolled on top of her and took her lips in a surprisingly gentle kiss.

The kiss spoke not so much of hot, unbridled desire and greedy want, but rather of something deeper, something beautiful and caring that made Layla want him more than ever.

She opened her thighs to welcome him and he slid deep into her with a sigh. For a long moment neither of them moved. She clung to him, her arms wrapped around his back as their heartbeats mirrored each other in a wild rhythm.

He began to move then, slowly and with long deep strokes that began the rise of a new tension inside her. All her nerve endings were enflamed and she arched beneath him seeking another release. When it came she cried out his name and realized he was there, too, crashing back to earth as he whispered her name.

Almost immediately he got up from the bed. "Are you coming back?" she asked. "Please come back," she added.

"All right," he replied simply and then left the bedroom.

She got out of bed and grabbed her nightgown and pulled it on over her head and then got back beneath the warm sheets that smelled of Jacob.

She hoped he'd come back to the bedroom. She wanted him to have the comfort of the bed for the night. She also wanted him to hold her close to him until she drifted off to sleep.

Her heart swelled as he returned and slid back beneath the sheets. She snuggled next to him, pleased as he turned on his side and pulled her against his chest.

"Now I suppose you're going to do a verbal replay of everything just so I can hear the sound of your voice." His voice held a relaxed, teasing tone.

"Hmm, actually, the whole experience has left me rather speechless," she replied.

"I hope that's speechless in a good way."

"Definitely. If I was a cat I'd be purring."

He stroked a hand down her thigh. "And if you were a bunny the possibilities would be endless."

She laughed. "Why, Agent Grayson, nobody mentioned to me that you actually have a sense of humor."

"There was a time some people thought I was quite witty."

Layla inched away from him and propped herself up on her elbow so she could see his face in the fading light that whispered through the window. "Tell me about the women in your past. Were there hundreds?"

He laughed, the sound deep and pleasant. "No, just a few. The last couple of years I'd focused almost exclusively on work."

"Any heartbreak in that few?"

"What, are we playing Twenty Questions?" he protested.

"I will if you want to, but it might just be easier to appease my naturally curious nature." She reached out and shoved a strand of his dark hair from his forehead, unable to fight her need to touch him.

"There was one," he said. "But doesn't everyone have at least one heartbreak in their past?"

She frowned thoughtfully. "I don't. I have a lot of broken relationships, but I'm not sure my heart has really been broken before. I just refuse to allow that to happen."

She was too embarrassed to admit to him that the men in her life didn't stick around long enough for her to become truly emotionally involved with them.

"So, tell me about this woman who broke your heart," she said, wanting to know everything about him.

He pulled her back into his arms and kissed her on the forehead. "We were young, she was pretty and I thought it was love, but she was just having fun. It seemed like a big deal at the time, but not so much now."

"Is she why you decided not to do relationships?"

"Enough, Layla. Enough talk for one night."

"You know there's really only one way to shut me up," she said as she allowed her fingers to smooth down the flat of his abdomen and down to his inner thigh.

He drew in a breath and chuckled. "I had a feeling there might be a little bit of bunny in you," he said softly just before his mouth claimed hers.

It was almost an hour later that Jacob slept with her curled up in his arms. The howl of the wind outside sounded bitterly cold and lonely, but she was warm and sweetly sated next to Jacob.

He just might become her very first real heartbreak, she thought as the wind rattled the glass in the window frame. He'd walk away from her when this was all over just like all the other men she'd slept with or dated. But, this time she had a feeling it was going to hurt more than it ever had before.

She closed her eyes as sleep threatened to overcome her. One thing was certain, in the future whenever she needed to go to a safe and happy place in her mind, she'd come back to this moment in his arms.

He was a patient man. The Professional sat in his favorite chair and listened to the wind screeching outside his windows while he took a sip of hot cocoa.

He knew Jacob Grayson had Layla stashed someplace

here in town and it was just a matter of time before he found them. The others were hidden in a place he was confident they wouldn't be found, and as far as he was concerned he was above suspicion anyway.

Smarter than the FBI, better than the local yokels, he could have made Black Rock his hunting ground forever, but after his party he'd be gone. Like a shadow in the night, like a phantom in a dream, he'd disappear and set up shop in another place.

As the howling wind got more intense, he decided he'd go someplace where it was warm. Maybe Florida or California. He smiled at the thought of all those beach bunnies just waiting to be plucked for a party.

Yes, it was time to head to a warmer climate, but first he had to get to Layla West. Then the real fun would begin.

It was snowing when Jacob got out of bed the next morning. Not a pretty, gentle fall of flakes, but a wheezing, icy blizzard. It must have started several hours before because the ground already sported at least two inches.

"Terrific," he muttered drily. This would only hurt the investigation, making the search more difficult.

He poured himself a cup of coffee and then moved back to the window, grateful that Layla was still asleep. He'd awakened spooned around her warm body. Before he opened his eyes to face the day he'd been happy.

Frowning, he felt a restless adrenaline try to take

hold of him. He wanted to be investigating instead of cooped up here in the cabin. He knew protecting Layla was important, but right now an edge of impatience, of urgency, filled him.

He suspected these new emotions were in response to his growing feelings for the woman in the next room. He didn't want to care about her, but he did and with each minute that passed, each hour that went by, that feeling grew stronger.

She'd made it clear to him that she wasn't the marrying kind, and he knew that his involvement with her could only lead to a new kind of heartbreak, but he didn't know how to protect himself from her.

She was bigger than life with her infectious laughter and depth of compassion. He knew she was loyal to her friends and had a side that was very nurturing. She'd make a good mother.

Again he frowned as he thought of her plan to be a single parent. No man? No problem. That had been her attitude. She didn't need a partner, wasn't in the market for one. In this particular aspect she reminded him of the woman he'd thought he'd once loved.

As he stared out to the drifting, blowing snow he realized his love for Sarah hadn't been as deep as he'd thought. Sure, he'd enjoyed her company and there had definitely been an element of lust involved. A marriage proposal had seemed like the obvious next step in their relationship, but he was grateful now that Sarah had turned him down.

It felt like fate that he was here now with Layla, but he reminded himself not to get used to it, that she was a temporary woman in a temporary situation and he'd do well to remember that.

By the time she got up he'd worked himself into a foul mood. She saw the snow as a wintry delight and he saw it only as an impediment to them getting out of the cabin for good.

His thoughts were echoed by Tom, who called just after nine. "I was hoping to set up a face-to-face meeting with you and the three men we discussed the other day. Unfortunately, this weather has thrown a wrench in the plans."

"Yeah, I figured," Jacob replied, trying to ignore the jiggle of Layla's bottom as she whipped eggs in a bowl. This morning she was dressed in a pair of black jeans and a white-and-black striped sweater that clung to every curve she possessed.

"Michael Fields turned out to be a dead end," Tom continued.

"Michael Fields?" Jacob frowned, for a moment unable to place the name.

"The man in unit seven at the motel who wanted Layla to show him property," Tom reminded him. "Turns out he's from Texas. He's retiring and he and his wife are looking at several small towns to relocate. They'd driven through Black Rock in the fall and were charmed. We checked him out thoroughly and he has solid alibis for all the kidnappings."

"So, that's one name to strike off our very short list of suspects," Jacob said in frustration.

"Jacob, we're doing everything we can."

"I know, I know," Jacob replied hurriedly. "I'm just getting cabin fever." He left the kitchen and walked into the living room. "I feel the need to be more involved. I want to find this creep and I can't do it from here."

He needed some distance from Layla, who was making him breakfast like she had every morning they'd been cooped up here. He needed to escape the domestic life they were building day by day, a life that was far too appealing.

"There's nothing that can be done today," Tom said. "We even had to call off the search because of the weather. It's supposed to clear up by nightfall. Maybe tomorrow I can get you in here for those interviews. You're the only person who has talked to this madman and I'm hoping something will come from that."

"Let's hope," Jacob agreed. By the time the two men had hung up Layla had French toast ready for them.

She was unusually quiet during the meal and he found himself wanting to know her thoughts. "Why so quiet?" he finally asked.

She poured more syrup over her French toast and didn't meet his gaze. "I feel like I'm keeping you from the rest of your life, from doing what you really want to do."

He realized she'd been listening to his conversation

with Tom and she was hurt. His heart softened. "Layla, look at me."

Slowly, as if with great reluctance, she met his gaze and in the depths of her beautiful blue eyes he saw a whisper of pain, an edge of guilt.

"If it wasn't for you I'd still be wallowing in self-pity and drinking myself into an early grave," he said. "You brought me back to life." As he said the words he recognized the truth of them and saw the lightening of her eyes.

"Really?"

"Really," he replied. Once again he felt he was getting too close, feeling too much for her. He cleared his throat and focused back on his breakfast.

He'd made love to her the night before and already he felt the burn of desire for her once again. He needed to get out of here, needed some distance from her. But there was nowhere to go to escape her presence in the small cabin.

She was everywhere, in every corner of every room, her scent in the very air he breathed. He had to focus. He sat down in the recliner and picked up one of the files on the missing women. Suzy Bakersfield had been taken after her shift as a cocktail waitress at The Edge.

Her car had been left out front of the bar and for several days the speculation was that she'd met some man and gone off with him, even though Suzy's current boyfriend had insisted that wasn't true.

Jennifer Hightower, the first missing young woman,

had been taken after she'd finished work at a local convenience store. And speculation was that Casey Teasdale had been taken early in the morning as she'd gotten into her car to go to work. The crime scene in all cases had been the women's cars, but other than the button in Casey's car, nothing else had been found. And there was no way to know for sure if that button was even connected to the crime.

He barely glanced up as Layla came into the room and sank down on the sofa. She pulled out the journal he knew she kept and began to write in it. She wrote for only a brief time and then closed the journal, set it on the coffee table and looked at him.

"Jacob, if you need to do something besides sit around here all day and babysit me, I'm okay with that. I could spend time with Portia or I'd even be all right staying here alone."

He eyed her in disbelief.

"Seriously," she exclaimed. "He doesn't know we're here and there's no reason to believe that he'll find us if we continue to be careful."

There was no question in Jacob's mind that The Professional didn't know their location. If he did know, something would have happened by now, another attempt would have been made on Layla.

"It's a moot point right now," he replied and gestured toward the window. "Nobody is going anywhere today."

"But I want you to know that you're free to do what

you need to do to catch this man. And if that means working the case outside of this cabin, then so be it."

He looked for signs of fear in her eyes, in her features, but saw no indication of that emotion. "Why the change of heart? It was only yesterday you were terrified when I disappeared for a few minutes to get that Christmas tree."

She shifted her gaze away from his and sighed. "I'm tired, Jacob. I'm tired of being here. I want my life back. I want my cat. We can't stay here forever. I mean, what if this killer doesn't do anything for weeks, for months?"

She sat up taller and straightened her shoulders. "As long as he's out there the women in this town are in danger. You know this killer better than anyone else because of your previous contact with him. Therefore, you're the best chance we have of catching him. You need to be actively working this case, not sitting in that chair reading the facts from a file."

She continued to surprise him. "We'll see," he replied. "I'm hoping to meet with the three men who have recently moved to Black Rock at Tom's office to see if something about their speech patterns is familiar to me." He glanced toward the window once again. "Hopefully I can do that in the next day or two."

"And while you do that I'll see if Portia wants to hang out," she replied. "I just want this over," she said firmly.

Jacob stared back down at the folder in his lap. She was ready to move on, he thought. She was probably tired of his company, eager to get back to real life and other men.

He jumped as his cell phone rang. He pulled it from his pocket and checked the caller ID. An unrecognized number. Jacob answered.

"Good morning, Jacob," The Professional's altered voice came across the line. "Are you enjoying this wintry weather?"

"What do you want?" Jacob asked, his stomach tightening with tension.

"Ah, surely you remember that I'm a sociable kind of man."

"Why don't you give me a name?" Jacob asked. "Your first name."

The caller laughed. "And why would I want to do that?"

"Just to be sociable," Jacob replied.

Again he laughed and Jacob tried to memorize the sound. "I just wanted to let you know that I bought party favors the other day. You know, that kind that you blow in and a long tongue of paper comes out."

"Tell me where you have those women," Jacob said, aware of Layla getting off the sofa and moving to crouch by his side.

"No can do," the caller replied.

"Then tell me your first name," Jacob pressed, his voice louder than he'd meant it to be. Layla placed a hand on his thigh, as if to calm him.

"You're as tenacious as a terrier. My name is The Professional and that's all you need to know."

"You say you want to play a game, but a game isn't fair unless there are clues."

"Who said I play fair?" His voice was filled with a smug amusement that ripped at Jacob's insides.

"Invite me to your party, you spineless creep," he exclaimed, unable to control the frustration that roiled inside of him. Layla's fingernails dug into his jeans and he drew a deep steadying breath. "Why don't you meet me someplace and we'll party together, just the two of us."

"Sorry, you're just not my type," The Professional replied and then clicked off the line.

Jacob closed his phone and muttered a curse beneath his breath.

"He just calls to stir you up," Layla said softly. "He calls to get under your skin because he knows he can. He feeds off you. Maybe you shouldn't take his calls anymore." She took his hand in hers, the warmth of the touch soothing his ragged nerves.

"I have to take the calls," he replied. "In one of them he might slip up. He might say something that will be a real clue to his identity."

He was grateful when she dropped his hand and returned to her place on the sofa, grateful because he'd liked the feel of her hand in his and knew that she had been offering him support.

And even though he hadn't believed he'd gotten

involved with her, even though he'd warned himself not to get emotionally attached, he realized that once this was all over, Layla West would leave a new scar on his heart.

Chapter 10

The weather in Kansas was crazy. The snow stopped falling midafternoon and the sun came out in all its glory, quickly melting what had fallen.

By the next morning there were only patches of snow left around tree trunks and in the thickest part of the woods that surrounded the cabin.

Layla stood at the bedroom window and stared outside, her thoughts on the man in the next room. They'd made love again the night before. It had just happened…the spark of passion, the uncontrollable need to be in each other's arms. It had been sheer magic.

It was getting more and more difficult for her to pretend that she didn't care about him, more difficult to maintain the distance that had always served her so well when it came to men.

She didn't want to get involved with him, and more than that she didn't want to feel any hope of a future with him. She knew she'd only be deluding herself and would ultimately be devastated.

Tom had called to let Jacob know he'd set up a two o'clock meeting with Jerry Tipton, the traveling salesman, and a two-thirty with Greg Todd, the nurse. He'd also set up a four o'clock meeting with Larry Norwood at his house because he was not working at his office that day.

Jacob appeared in the bedroom doorway. "Ready?"

She nodded and picked up her purse from the bed. "I'll spend the day with Portia at the daycare and she can bring me back here around five."

He frowned but said nothing as they left the cabin and headed for the shed. She'd insisted that Portia bring her back here rather than have Jacob drive out to the Norwood place and then back into town to get her and then back to the cabin.

"You know I don't mind backtracking to pick you up."

"I know, but this works out better. We'll be careful and make sure we aren't followed and everything will be fine," she assured him. She needed to prove to herself that she could be okay without him for a little while. It wasn't like she was going to spend the night there all alone. It would probably only be a matter of minutes that she would be by herself.

They were silent on the ride into town. Layla suspected Jacob had already gone into investigation mode, that his thoughts were consumed by the need to crack this case, save his sister and the other women and then get on with his own life, wherever it might take him.

"I'll see you back at the cabin," he said as he pulled up in the driveway of Portia's gingerbread-trimmed house.

"I just hope the next time we talk you know who The Professional is and he's behind bars," she said as she opened the truck door.

For a moment the demons were back in his eyes and she wanted to climb back in the truck and wrap her arms around him, she wanted to say something that would put a glint of laughter there. Instead she got out of the truck and closed the door.

He remained parked in the driveway until she reached the door to the detached garage where Portia's daycare business resided.

As she turned to wave to him, she was gripped by a sudden, inexplicable sense of dread. She told herself it was just because this was the first time they'd been separated since the attack on her in her office.

Portia and the kids quickly took away any disquiet she felt. The afternoon sped by with plenty of kisses and hugs and laughter. Layla gave herself completely to the joy of being with the kids, but couldn't help but wonder what life would be like if she was together with Jacob and had his baby. She knew instinctively that he would be a wonderful father.

"I'm in love with him," she confessed to Portia as the two of them went into Portia's private office. Portia's assistant was having reading time with the children, which gave Portia and Layla time for a little girl talk.

"Are you sure you don't feel that way because of the circumstances you find yourself in?" Portia asked. "There's no question that Jacob represents safety for you. Maybe you're just confused about your feelings for him?"

Layla considered her words. "There's no question that he makes me feel safe and secure," she agreed. "But he's also passionate about things and has a wonderful sense of humor, and even if there was no danger at all in my life I'd be in love with him."

"Does he feel the same way about you?"

"I'm sure he doesn't," Layla replied with a wistful pang in her heart. "He's physically attracted to me, but you know that's always the easy part for me. Men want to take me to bed but they never want to marry me." She forced a smile to her lips. "Don't look so concerned. Once this is all over Jacob will just be another passing ship in my life and I'll be fine."

Portia looked at the clock on her wall. "And if you want to stop by the vet's office and visit Mr. Whiskers, we'd better get out of here." She got out of her chair and grabbed her coat and purse while Layla did the same.

She'd asked Portia to run her by to see her kitty on the way home. She desperately missed the cat and hoped he wasn't grieving over the separation from her. She knew seeing that he was being well cared for would ease her heart.

"So, are you going to tell Jacob how you feel about him?" Portia asked when they were in her car and headed to Main Street.

"No. What's the point?" Layla countered. "If he wants something to happen between us then he'll tell me. I definitely don't want to get my hopes up and be disappointed again. It's easier to have no expectations than to have them crushed."

"Sometimes I think that's your problem," Portia replied. "That you have no expectations for yourself or your happiness. You just assume you won't be happy, won't be loved, and so it doesn't happen for you."

"Please, let's not turn this into another counseling session," Layla exclaimed with a small laugh.

"You should have had counseling years ago because of the abuse from your father," Portia retorted.

"I don't need counseling," Layla replied. "I survived and I'm doing just fine." She put a note of finality in her voice, hoping Portia would drop the whole subject.

Thankfully by that time Portia had pulled up and parked in front of Larry Norwood's veterinarian office. "Are you coming in?" Layla asked as she opened the car door.

"Are you going to be long?"

Layla shook her head. "Not at all. Why don't you sit tight and keep the car running and warm? I know Larry isn't here today so it should just take me a couple of minutes to check on my baby."

Portia frowned and Layla knew she was probably remembering the last time she'd let Layla go off alone. "I'll be fine," she exclaimed to her friend as she got out of the car and shut the door.

Once inside the office she was greeted by Margaret Wisong, the receptionist. "Dr. Larry isn't in today," she said after greeting Layla.

"I know, I was just wondering if I could have a quick visit with my cat, Mr. Whiskers," Layla explained.

"Oh, my, that cat is a lover." Margaret smiled and gestured to exam room one. "Why don't you go in there and I'll bring him to you."

The examining room was typical, with a sink and cabinets and a stainless steel table. Margaret came in carrying Mr. Whiskers and as Layla took the cat from her arms, he began to purr loudly.

"I've missed you, too," Layla murmured as she stroked his soft fur and cuddled him like a baby against her chest. "Is he eating okay?" she asked Margaret.

"No problems, and he's sleeping fine, too," Margaret assured her. "And don't worry, he's getting plenty of play with everyone here. He's become one of our favorites."

"Good," Layla replied. "It won't be too much longer and you can come home," she said to the cat. She felt better now, knowing that he was doing fine. "Thanks for taking such good care of him," she said to Margaret.

"No problem." Margaret took the cat from Layla's arms. "We love taking care of doggies and kitties," she said. "Is there anything else I can do for you?"

"No thanks, I was just feeling a little homesick for my cat," Layla replied.

As Margaret left the examining room Layla started to follow behind her. She had no idea what made her glance at the white lab coat hanging from a hook in the corner, but her gaze fell on the sleeve and the row of decorative oversize white buttons on the cuff.

Her heart stuttered to a near stop as she saw that one of those buttons was missing, a button that looked just like the one that had been found in Casey Teasdale's car.

Larry Norwood. Her brain fought to make sense of it. He could have lost that button anywhere, she tried to rationalize. On wooden legs she left the examining room. Or he could have lost it in a struggle with Casey Teasdale.

Was it possible the friendly vet was the monster they sought?

She felt half-dizzy, sick to her stomach. *Don't jump to any conclusions,* she told herself. There might be several people in town who wore those kinds of lab coats. But even as she told herself this her heart thundered with the weight of her discovery.

Once outside she slid into the passenger side of Portia's car. "Everything all right with Mr. Whiskers?" Portia asked.

"Fine. Everything is fine," Layla replied. She was bursting with the need to tell Portia what she'd seen, but she was afraid to involve her friend. She didn't want to malign the vet if he wasn't guilty.

Besides, she didn't want anyone to know until she had a chance to tell Jacob. He'd know what to do. He'd be able to clear the vet or make sure that Norwood was put behind bars if he was guilty.

She glanced at her wristwatch and saw that it was quarter to four. He'd be on his way to the Norwood farm to interrogate the vet. As soon as Portia dropped her at the cabin she'd call him.

Layla pulled her journal and a pen from her purse. Portia glanced her way and grinned. "Are you still journaling all the time?"

"Every day," Layla replied. "Sorry, I just need to make a quick note to myself." She jotted down the words *Larry Norwood, missing button, lab coat* and then closed the small book, some of the pressure of the secret diminished just by writing it down.

The drive seemed to last forever. Portia chatted about her pregnancy, the kids in her daycare and Caleb. Thankfully, she didn't seem to notice that Layla was unusually quiet, her thoughts consumed by the possibility that Larry could be The Professional.

Where had Larry and his family lived before coming to Black Rock? Hadn't he moved here about the same time that the case in Kansas City had wrapped up? She wished she had the answers, and she definitely wished she knew how he'd lost the button on his lab coat.

Maybe she'd just found the clue they needed to crack the case. Surely Tom and Jacob would be able to match the missing button on the lab coat to the one found in the car.

"Are you sure you'll be okay here by yourself until Jacob gets home?" Portia asked as she parked in front of the cabin. "I could hang around until he gets back."

"Absolutely not," Layla replied. "Besides, you mentioned earlier that you have a parent-teacher meeting to get back to."

"I could call the parents and cancel," Portia said. "I just wanted to talk to them about their little boy's penchant for hair-pulling."

"Nonsense, go to your meeting. I'll be fine until Jacob gets home." Besides, if what she suspected was true, then she didn't have to worry about Larry Norwood finding her. He was at this very moment being questioned by Jacob and Tom.

"Thanks for letting me spend the afternoon with you," she said as she got out of the car.

"You know I always love spending time with you. Take care, Layla, and I'll talk to you later."

Layla's heart still thundered as she watched Portia pull away. Larry Norwood! She couldn't believe it, but the evidence didn't lie.

She turned and hurried up the steps to the cabin. Once

inside she pulled her journal from her purse and carried it with her into the kitchen and the phone.

She picked up the receiver and frowned. "Hello?" Her stomach plummeted. There was no dial tone. The phone was dead. It was at that moment she knew she was in deep trouble.

She turned to run into the living room to get her purse and her cell phone when the back door that led into the kitchen exploded open and her nightmare grinned behind his mask. "Hi, honey. I'm home," he said as Layla screamed.

The interview with Jerry Tipton and Greg Todd had been another study in frustration. Jacob and Tom were silent as Jacob drove toward the Norwood farm on the outskirts of town.

"Greg Todd is some piece of work, isn't he?" Tom finally broke the silence.

"Arrogant young kid with an attitude as bad as his complexion," Jacob replied. "But, he's not smart enough to be our man."

"Why would somebody that age decide to move to a little town like Black Rock?" Tom asked.

"My guess would be he was having trouble getting hired in the bigger hospitals."

"What about Tipton?" Tom leaned forward and adjusted the heat vent to blow more directly on his body.

Jacob thought about the traveling salesman who had seemed very eager to cooperate, but had been unable to provide any real alibis for the times of the kidnapping. "I think we need to look closer at him. Check his financials and see if we can pin down where he was and when. He has the perfect job to fit the profile and he seemed bright to me."

"And way too eager to please," Tom added. "Did you notice how he kept wanting to know all the details about the crimes?"

"Could be morbid curiosity or something more malevolent," Jacob replied. "I know it's not unusual for these guys to try to insinuate themselves into the investigation. What frustrates me is that I didn't pick up anything in their voices or speech patterns that made me believe one of them was The Professional." He tightened his hands on the steering wheel.

He just wanted this over. He wanted Brittany and the other women safe and sound, wanted the killer dead or behind bars and needed to get Layla out of the cabin and out of his life.

Because he wanted her in his life.

He shook his head as if to dislodge that particular thought. He couldn't want her because she didn't need a man. She was just another heartache as far as he was concerned and he'd suffered a lifetime of heartbreaks in this life already.

"You know, it's possible these three are just dead ends," Jacob said. "He might not even be on our radar at this point."

"Don't remind me." Tom's voice held the same kind of weariness that Jacob felt.

Jacob felt like he'd spent his entire life chasing this killer and he feared that once again they wouldn't find him in time and there would be another party to clean up after.

His stomach twisted as he thought of the killer's last party and that his sister might be a part of the next one. No, they couldn't let that happen.

"He's just not making mistakes," Jacob finally growled and slammed a hand down on the steering column. "And we need the bastard to make a mistake before we lose Brittany, before we lose them all."

A wealth of despair filled Jacob and pressed so tight against his chest he could scarcely draw a breath. He felt as if they were running out of time. He knew that eventually The Professional would no longer be able to control his compulsion to kill.

As far as Jacob was concerned they were already on borrowed time. He'd tried to act on his compulsion both times he'd attempted to kidnap Layla. He should be ready to explode at any moment, like a bomb that killed everything and everyone in his path.

Not Brittany, he thought. *Please, not Brittany and not Layla.* Somehow they had to stop this man before more women died, before more families were destroyed by grief and despair.

"What are your plans when this is all over?" Tom asked, pulling Jacob from his inner torment.

"I plan on staying here in Black Rock. I'm kind of hoping there will be an opening for a deputy." He slid a glance to his brother.

"With Benjamin quitting in the spring I'm sure we could use you, but are you sure you don't want to go back to the FBI? You could. Your supervisor has kept in touch with me."

Jacob once again looked at Tom, this time in surprise. "He has?"

"He was worried about you and told me that when you were ready to let you know you still have a job there if you want it."

Jacob digested this information and then shook his head. "No, as much as I appreciate knowing that, I won't go back. I'm not cut out for the kind of work I was doing. I allow myself to get too emotionally involved."

"That particular trait is highly desired in one of my deputies," Tom replied. "You know there's nothing we'd all like better than to have you here. But I wanted you to know that you have options."

"Thanks," he replied, but he'd already made up his mind that he wanted to stay in Black Rock. He hadn't realized how homesick he'd been until he'd come back here. He hadn't recognized the depth of his loneliness in Kansas City until he'd returned here to the warmth and caring of his family.

He knew that if he went back to the FBI he'd immerse himself in his work and would probably never build a life that included a real home and family. He was stunned to realize he wanted that.

He wanted a woman to come home to, somebody who would force him to eat breakfast because it was the most important meal of the day, somebody who would warm his nights and brighten his days. He wanted a woman who talked too much and loved high-heeled shoes, a woman exactly like Layla.

As he turned into the long winding driveway of the Norwood place, he shoved everything out of his head except the investigation.

On paper Larry Norwood looked the least likely to be a serial killer. He was a successful businessman with a wife and two children and was well-respected in the community. But Jacob reminded himself that John Wayne Gacy had been a beloved and respected member of his community who dressed up like a clown to entertain his friends and neighbors, and he'd killed thirty-three young men and boys.

The killer's profile was only as good as the paper it was written on and there was always room for error.

The Norwood home was a small, neat ranch. A bright red barn sat near the house, along with a gardening shed. Beyond the house was a rolling rise of pasture.

The barn was too close to the main residence to house the missing women, Jacob thought as he parked the car and turned off the engine.

"This doesn't look promising," he muttered.

"If nothing else, after this interview 'Norwood' is a

name we can cross off our list of potential suspects," Tom reminded him.

The two men got out of the truck and Jacob felt the bite of the cold north wind. The slight respite they'd had of winter weather that had quickly melted the snow was gone, replaced by the promise of another storm soon to arrive.

Tension twisted Jacob's gut as he and Tom approached the house. They needed answers and he felt as if they were spinning their wheels while time ran out for the victims.

Tom knocked on the door and as they waited for a reply Jacob once again scanned the immediate area. The barn door was open, indicating that there were probably no secrets inside. He turned back to face the door as it opened.

An attractive blonde offered them a tentative smile. Two little girls peeked out from behind her. "Sheriff Grayson, didn't Larry call you?"

"Call me about what?" Tom asked.

"He got an emergency call about a sick horse and had to leave. He said he was going to let you know." She looked from Tom to Jacob. "He must have forgotten. I'm sorry about the inconvenience."

"Do you know who called him about the horse?" Jacob asked.

She shook her head. "No, I'm sorry I don't." She hesitated a moment, and then continued. "Would you like to come in and wait for him?" It was obvious she was uncomfortable with the idea of the two men coming inside.

"We'll just hang out in the truck for a little while and see if he shows up," Tom replied. "If he happens to check in with you would you get his location for us?"

"Of course. I'm sure he won't be too long." With another smile she closed the door and Jacob heard the click of a lock being turned.

"You can't blame her for being cautious," Jacob said as they walked back to the truck. "For all she knows we're the men who are responsible for the disappearances of the women. Just because we have a badge doesn't mean we're the good guys."

Once they were in the truck Jacob looked at his watch. "Maybe I should call Layla and let her know I'm going to be later than I thought." He pulled his phone from his pocket and punched in the numbers to her cell phone, then frowned as it went directly to her voice mail.

"No answer?" Tom asked as Jacob hung up.

"It went to her voice mail." An uneasy tension began to build inside him.

"She and Portia are probably in the middle of shopping or talking and Layla didn't hear the phone," Tom said as if to assure Jacob.

"Maybe." Jacob punched in the numbers to the phone inside the cabin, but hung up after it rang four times without an answer. Surely Tom was right. She was with

Portia and hadn't yet made it to the cabin. He hoped that was the case, for any other scenario was absolutely unthinkable.

Chapter 11

Layla screamed as the man advanced on her. She turned and ran from the kitchen, terror shouting in her head as her heart raced frantically.

She knew there was no place to hide in either the living room or the bedroom, so she headed for the bathroom, where she could at least lock the door.

She flew into the small room, twisted the lock and only then released the sob of horror that had welled up inside her. If she could just stay safe until Jacob got home.

Confusion played in her mind. She'd been so certain that Larry Norwood was The Professional, but Jacob and Tom were interviewing Larry, so he couldn't be the man in the house. So who had broken in the back door? Who was behind that mask?

A loud bang resounded on the bathroom door and a scream once again clawed up her throat. She stared at the door, her entire body suffused with a trembling that kept her frozen in place.

"Come out, come out, Layla," a deep voice called from the other side of the door.

Instantly she was cast back in time. She was a little girl hiding under the porch, hoping and praying that she wouldn't be found. The trembling inside her grew more intense and she slid down the wall as tears began to flow down her cheeks.

Don't let him get me, a childish voice whispered urgently in her head. *Please don't let him get me.* Ancient fear mixed with present terror, making it difficult for her to draw a breath, to think clearly.

She tried to think of what she'd done to garner his violence. Had she washed the dishes wrong? Had her bed not been made properly? She'd tried so hard to be good, but it was never good enough.

She shook her head. No, this wasn't about her father. This was about The Professional. There was no sound on the other side of the door. Rather than the silence making her feel better, it horrified her.

What was he doing? Surely he wouldn't just give up so easily and just go away. Her sobs halted as she caught her breath and waited in dreadful anticipation. Every nerve in her body screamed. Every muscle she possessed tensed.

A bang sounded on the door and the wood in the center cracked, exposing an ax blade. Layla jumped to her feet in panicked horror.

She fought through her fear, knowing that if she froze she was dead, that if she stopped thinking she would be his last victim. The window!

With adrenaline-fueled strength she raced to the small window and gasped in relief as it slid open easily. As the ax slammed into the door again and again she punched out the screen and began to climb outside.

She almost made it. Her upper body was outside when he crashed into the bathroom and grabbed one of her legs. She kicked and twisted to get free, unable to summon the strength to scream again as she fought to get free.

She kicked so hard she felt as if she'd thrown her leg out of the socket, but she was rewarded by a gruff grunt and suddenly she was free and falling to the ground.

Run!

She hit the frozen earth hard, her breath whooshing out of her. She got to her feet and took off, praying she could get to Benjamin and Edie's house before the masked man caught her.

She'd gone only a few feet when she realized she'd lied to Jacob. There were some things she couldn't do in high heels, like run fast enough to escape a serial killer.

She kicked off the shoes, not breaking her pace as she ran for her life.

His laughter rang in the air, far too close behind her. Tears blurred her vision as the cold ground froze her bare feet. *Don't look,* her mind screamed. *Don't waste the time to turn and look behind you.*

She didn't look but she felt him, felt the malevolence rolling off him as he closed the gap between them. She wasn't going to make it. Sobs ripped inside her chest. She wasn't going to get to safety.

He grabbed her then, pulled her down by the shoulders. Once again she hit the ground and rolled, still trying to get some distance from him.

He jumped on her, laughing once again as if it were all nothing more than a game to him. "That's it, fight me," he exclaimed as he managed to straddle her chest with her arms trapped beneath his legs. "There's nothing I love better than a good fight."

She would have continued to fight, but at that moment she recognized his voice. She'd been right. "Larry? Larry, what are you doing?"

Without warning he slapped her, the blow ringing bells in her ears and scorching her cheek with stinging heat. "My name is The Professional and don't you forget it."

Layla watched in horror as he pulled a hypodermic needle from his pocket. "Please, no," she begged, even though she knew her pleas would fall on deaf ears.

The sting of the needle in her arm was nothing compared to the ache in her heart as she thought of Jacob. She'd never see him again. She'd never know the glory of being held in his arms, of tasting his lips against hers just one last time.

It was over. This was the end. Her life was over and it was Jacob's beautiful face that filled her mind as darkness overwhelmed her.

Jacob checked his watch for the tenth time in twenty minutes and then sighed in frustration. "I say we go home and arrange to meet Dr. Norwood another time. For all we know it could be hours before he gets back here."

"You're right," Tom said, sounding as defeated as Jacob felt. "I'll call him in the morning and see if we can meet with him then."

Jacob nodded. He was eager to get back to the cabin. He'd tried to call Layla several more times but she hadn't answered.

A thrum of anxiety had begun inside him and with each minute that passed it grew more intense. The only reason he wasn't completely in panic mode was because he'd tried to call Portia and she hadn't answered her phone, either. He could only assume it was possible the two were still together and had their phones buried in their purses or shut off altogether.

"You know the number of Portia's daycare?" he asked Tom. "I'll call there and see if maybe they haven't even left there yet."

Tom rattled off the number and Jacob called. "Portia," he exclaimed with a sense of relief when she answered. "It's Jacob. Can I talk to Layla?"

"She isn't here, Jacob," Portia replied with a touch of unease in her voice. "I dropped her at the cabin about thirty minutes ago."

A new sense of urgency swept through him. "Thanks." He clicked off and shoved the truck into gear. "Something's wrong at the cabin. Portia said she dropped Layla off thirty minutes ago."

He roared down the road that led away from the Norwood farm, his heart stuttering wildly in his chest. Why wasn't she answering her phone? What the hell was going on?

"Don't jump to conclusions," Tom said. "Maybe she's in the shower or taking a nap and hasn't heard the phone."

"Maybe." Jacob tightened his hands on the steering wheel. He didn't believe she was showering or napping. All his instincts were screaming that Layla was in trouble. Jesus, he should have left the Norwood place the first time he'd called and been unable to reach her.

Ignoring the legal limits he stomped on the gas pedal, wishing he had wings to fly at the speed of sound. Tom said nothing and for that Jacob was grateful. He didn't want to listen to all the logical reasons why Layla wasn't answering the phone. He just wanted to get to her as quickly as possible.

"I wonder what kind of a horse emergency kept Norwood from the appointment?" Tom finally said.

Jacob shot him a quick, questioning glance. "You think there wasn't an emergency?"

Tom released a sigh of frustration. "I don't know what in the hell I think anymore."

Jacob's mind raced over everything he knew, everything he thought he knew about the killer. "In one of our phone conversations he told me I was as tenacious as a terrier. Sounds like a comparison a vet would use."

"That's speculation, not evidence," Tom reminded him.

Where was Larry Norwood? Was he really dealing with a sick horse or was he at the cabin now with Layla, planning his final move in the Black Rock area?

"I don't get it. Why would he blow off an interview with us when he knows we're going to check his alibi?" Tom said. "He knows he's on our radar, so why would he take chances like that?"

"I don't know. I can't think about it right now." As Jacob turned onto the Grayson property, the tension in his stomach twisted so tight he felt sick.

They flew past the big house, rocking over bumps in the lane as Jacob scarcely let up on the gas. He braked hard in front of the cabin, his heart pounding in dread as he then flew out of the truck.

Before he reached the porch he saw something bright and colorful lying on the ground on the side of the cabin. On leaden feet, his heart pounding so hard it hurt, he walked over and stared down at the pink-and-yellow-flowered high heel. He spied the second shoe nearby.

The ground spun beneath him and bile rose up in the back of his throat. *No.* The single word repeated itself over and over in his head. Had the shoes fallen off her feet as she'd been carried away by The Professional or had she taken them off to run? There was no way she'd just tossed the shoes outside for no reason.

Too late. The words pealed in his head like a bell gone mad. *Too late.* He was too late to save her, just like he'd been too late to save the others. "She's gone." The words fell like stones from his lips. It was his worst nightmare come true and he didn't know how to awaken from it.

Tom grabbed him by the arm. "Come on, let's check inside."

Both men drew their guns as they approached the cabin, even though in his heart Jacob knew The Professional wouldn't be inside. He was already planning his party, with Layla and Brittany as guests of honor.

When Jacob saw the shattered bathroom door and the ax lying on the floor next to it, he nearly fell to his knees in agony.

He couldn't imagine Layla's terror. A fine mist covered his sight as he thought of the utter fear she must have experienced. And he hadn't been here for her.

Damn him. Damn Larry Norwood and his sick, twisted mind. An edge of anger began to grow inside Jacob. He wouldn't blink if he got the opportunity to kill him.

It was easy to understand the chronology of events by the evidence left behind. He'd come through the back door. Layla must have run to the bathroom. The open window there indicated that she'd managed to crawl out and run, but she hadn't been able to run fast enough to escape her pursuer.

Numb. Jacob was numb as he and his brother stood in the kitchen and Tom called for help. He'd get men there to process the scene and others to search for Layla.

Jacob's gaze fell on the notebook laid open on the table. Layla's journal. He frowned. She never left it laying out where he could thumb through it. It was always in her purse.

He took a step closer and his heart nearly stopped once again as he read the words on the page. *Larry Norwood. Missing button. Lab coat.*

"Get somebody to Larry's office to collect all his lab coats," he told Tom, the numbness gone as he realized Layla had given them the clue they needed. It was all circumstantial, but it was enough for him to know that the friendly town vet was The Professional. "It's Larry."

Tom looked at the journal and a knot pulsed in his jaw. "Now all we have to do is find him before he kills anyone."

Flashbacks shot through Jacob's head, visions of dead women who would haunt him in some measure for the rest of his life. As Layla's face superimposed over the features of one of those women, he felt as if he'd been punched in the gut with a killing blow.

It was at that moment he realized the depth of his love for Layla, and what he feared more than anything was that he'd be too late for her, too. To make matters worse, it had begun to snow again.

Brittany sat up as the masked man carried in Layla West and placed the unconscious woman on the cot in the last cell. Her heart cried in anguish.

The cells were all full now and she knew that meant death wasn't far behind. She got up from her cot and grabbed the bars that held her prisoner as the man locked Layla's enclosure.

"My brothers will kill you for this," she said as he walked back toward the door.

He laughed. "Your brothers couldn't find a hole in the bottom of their socks." He pulled off his ski mask and she gasped in surprise as she realized it was Dr. Norwood.

She'd had little interaction with the vet before being taken by him. She also knew that he'd taken off the mask and allowed her to see who he was because he was certain there was no rescue for her or the others, that none of them would live to identify him to the authorities.

"They'll never stop looking for you," she replied with a lift of her chin. "They'll hunt you to the ends of the earth."

He laughed again. "They don't even know who I am, and by the time they figure it out I'll be long gone from Black Rock with a new identity and new hunting grounds."

"What about your wife and children?"

"What about them?" he replied. "They're nothing but a drain on my finances, a distraction I no longer want."

Cold. He was like a block of ice, a sociopath with no empathy, no feelings for anyone other than himself. She couldn't imagine now how he'd managed to maintain the facade of a caring veterinarian.

He gestured toward Layla. "She should be awake in just a little while and then we're going to have a party. I've got some special party favors out in the shed and I can't wait to share them with you all."

As he left the building Jennifer Hightower began to sob. "We're going to die. We're all going to die."

"No, we aren't," Brittany said vehemently. "You know what I'm going to do when I get out of here?" She didn't wait for a response. "I'm going to hire a carpenter to build a deck on the back of my house and when it's finished I'm going to throw a big barbecue and invite all my friends and family. Casey, what about you? What are you going to do when we get out of here?"

"I'm going to marry my boyfriend," she said. "He's asked me twice and both times I told him I wasn't ready. But when we get out of here I'm going to plan the biggest wedding this town has ever seen."

"I'm going to quit my job and go back to college," Suzy Bakersfield said. "I always wanted to be a lawyer, but I've been afraid to go for it. I'm ready to go for it now."

For a moment hope filled the air, a shining hope that Brittany grabbed on to and embraced in her heart, drew into her very soul. He might take their lives, but he'd never have their spirits or their dreams.

All too quickly that moment of peace was shattered as Layla moaned with the first stirring of consciousness. *She should be awake in just a little while and then we're going to have a party.* Larry's words whirled around in Brittany's brain and brought with them the hopeless despair of the doomed.

Chapter 12

Consciousness came in tiny bits and pieces. First Layla became aware of the aches of her body—her knees, her hips and finally her face. Everything hurt and she was reluctant to leave the sweet oblivion of the darkness behind for the cold harsh reality of the pain.

The second thing she became aware of was the fact that she was lying on a cot of some kind that smelled of mildew. She frowned, surfacing slowly into the here and now.

The last thing that pierced through her brain was voices…women's voices. They were soft whispers edged with fear and it was then total consciousness struck and Layla knew exactly where she was and what was happening to them all.

They were going to die. She didn't move, didn't open her eyes to let the others know she had awakened. She listened to them talking about all the things they were going to do when they escaped here and her heart felt heavier than it had ever felt in her life.

Jacob. He was an unfinished song in her heart, an ache in her very soul. She knew he'd blame himself for this, would probably retreat back into his self-destructive isolation and that broke her heart as much as the knowledge of her imminent death at the hands of Larry Norwood.

She'd never believed that they had a future together, but that didn't stop her heart aching with all the what-ifs.

"Layla?"

The soft voice drifted to her and she immediately recognized it as belonging to Brittany. "I'm here," she whispered.

"Are they looking for us? Do they have any idea who might be responsible?"

"Jacob should know by now," Layla replied. If he'd found her journal. If he'd bothered to read it. Oh, God, so many ifs to depend on for their rescue.

"Jacob? Isn't he in Kansas City?" Brittany asked. "At least he was there when I got abducted."

For the next few minutes Layla caught Brittany up on all the family news she'd missed while she'd been imprisoned.

As she talked, she realized how much she would have

loved being a part of the Grayson family, how much she would have loved to build a family with Jacob.

What she didn't share with the others was that Larry Norwood had committed this crime before and the result had been the deaths of five women. Even though she knew that they were aware of the danger they were in, she couldn't tell them about the real horror that was The Professional.

"Layla, when he comes back, you have to act like you're still unconscious," Brittany exclaimed. "It's the only thing that might buy us all some extra time."

"I can do that," Layla replied with an assurance she didn't feel. If he got too close to her he'd surely hear the pounding of her heart, the rapid breathing that she'd be unable to control. "Where are we?"

"We don't know," Suzy replied. "We've tried to figure it out, but we have no idea."

"For all we know we could be hundreds of miles from Black Rock," Casey added.

Layla looked at her wristwatch. It was just after six. "No, we're close to Black Rock," she said. She hadn't been unconscious very long. He must have used a light dose of the drug. *Couldn't wait to have his party,* she thought fearfully.

How long could she fake being totally drugged out? How much time could she buy them all before Larry lost his patience and started his sick party?

Remaining on the cot where she lay, Layla looked around, trying to figure out where they were being held.

It appeared to be a barn or some sort of shed that had been renovated for torture and imprisonment. Were they on property that belonged to Larry or somebody else?

Tom and Jacob had been to Larry's place that afternoon. Wouldn't they have noticed a big shed and gone to investigate?

As the only Realtor in the area she knew how many empty properties were around the town and knew that many of those places had structures just like this on them.

How were Jacob and the other men ever going to find the right place in time to save them? If it were humanly possible then she knew Jacob would be the man who could find them, but she wasn't sure it was possible.

As if to punctuate her dismal thoughts the door to the shed opened and he walked back in. Layla closed her eyes and focused on slowing the rhythm of her breathing, knowing that not only her life, but also the other women's lives might depend on her acting skills.

"No party is complete without balloons," he said. "And party favors, girls," he said. Layla tensed as she heard the sound of items being dropped on the floor, and Jennifer Hightower began to sob hysterically.

She couldn't even imagine what he'd brought in as "party favors" but she knew she had to keep her breathing slow and steady and not react to anything that might go on around her.

He began to whistle and she could tell from the

sound that he was approaching her cell. A rattle of keys indicated he was unlocking the door.

She considered springing up and attacking him. She'd have the element of surprise on her side, but quickly dismissed the idea as she remembered his strength and the fact that she was weak and banged up.

Instead she focused once again on playing dead, praying that she did nothing to let him know she was no longer unconscious.

The cell door squeaked open and she felt his presence next to her cot. *Stay focused,* she told herself as she drew in deep and even breaths. She kept her body boneless, her mouth slightly agape.

"Hey, Bozo," Brittany called out and Layla knew she was trying to distract him. "Why don't you open up my cage and fight with somebody who isn't drugged to the gills?"

He laughed and Layla nearly jumped out of her skin as she felt his breath on her face. Tears burned beneath her closed eyes, surged up in her chest and she feared if he remained so close to her for another second she'd lose it.

"I'm going to enjoy partying with you, Brittany," he said, his voice moving farther away from Layla. The door to her cell closed again. "But the party can't begin without Layla. She's been a real pain and I have special plans for her, but she has to be awake to really enjoy them."

She heard the scrape of chair legs against the floor.

"I'll just sit here and enjoy the atmosphere while we wait for Layla to join us," he said.

The only sound was the quiet sobbing of Jennifer and Casey and Larry's low melodic whistling as they all waited for the party to begin.

Jacob, where are you? Layla fought the emotion that threatened to erupt from her on a torrent of tears. *Please, find us,* she mentally begged. *Find us before it's too late.*

The snow that had begun as fat fluffy flakes had transformed into smaller, more serious frozen precipitation, only adding to Jacob's sense of urgency.

They were headed back to the Norwood farm, hoping to get answers there. The kid gloves were off as far as Jacob was concerned. If Larry wasn't there, then Jacob had some hard questions for Norwood's wife.

Benjamin was processing the cabin and before Tom and Jacob had left he'd picked up a couple of hairs just inside the back door that he suspected were dog hairs. They wouldn't know for sure until they were sent to the lab, but it was the final clue that Jacob needed to be certain that The Professional was, indeed, Larry Norwood.

They were in Tom's official car, with Tom at the wheel, leaving Jacob to clench his fists at his sides as he thought of Layla, of Brittany and all the other women who were in danger.

"How big is his property?" Jacob asked, knowing Tom

had asked Caleb to find out what property the Norwoods owned in the area.

"Almost two hundred acres."

"A big area," Jacob replied more to himself than to his brother. And the snow was falling and time had possibly already run out.

"I've got some men meeting us there. It's mostly pasture, so it shouldn't take us long to search."

Jacob said nothing. He knew an extra second, an added minute could mean the difference between life and death, and the thought of Layla no longer in this world nearly destroyed him.

He knew she wasn't interested in a long-term relationship. She hadn't even indicated to him that she felt anything about him except a flash of passion and perhaps some natural sympathy for all that he'd been through.

What surprised him was that he'd realized he was capable of loving again. Somehow in the past couple of days with Layla he'd rediscovered the hopes and dreams he'd believed were lost forever.

He might not have Layla in his life forever, but he wanted her in this world, needed to know she was alive and well even if she wasn't with him.

And he couldn't even think of his little sister in the hands of Larry Norwood. The rage of knowing the man had the two women Jacob cared about most in the world threatened to spiral him completely out of control. He knew he wouldn't be any use to anyone if he allowed that to happen. He had to stay in control, stay cool and calm despite his inner turmoil.

By the time they reached the Norwood place the snow had changed back to a hard-driving sleet that bounced off the windows and quickly slickened the roads.

Deputy Sam McCain and several others were already there waiting in their cars for Tom and Jacob's arrival. As Tom parked all of the men got out of their cars.

"Wait here," Tom instructed the others. "I'm hoping we can get Mrs. Norwood's permission to search the premises and just in case she balks Caleb is working at getting us a search warrant."

The last thing any of them wanted to do was gain evidence that a good criminal defense attorney would be able to get thrown out of court on a technicality. Jacob followed behind Tom as they approached the front door for the second time that day.

It was like déjà vu and memories from the last time he'd faced off with The Professional once again filled his head. That time the creep had won. But they couldn't let him win this time. This had to have a different ending, he prayed.

Larry's wife opened the door, her eyes widening as she saw the men standing in the yard. "Sheriff, what's going on?"

"Has Larry gotten home?" Tom asked.

"No, I haven't heard from him. Would somebody please tell me what's going on?" The fear that had widened her eyes now crept into her voice.

Behind her came the sounds of little-girl giggles and Jacob realized she and her daughters were just more victims of Larry's madness.

"Tracy, we need to get your permission to search your property," Tom explained. "We need to search both inside the house and outside."

"I don't understand. What are you looking for?"

"The women who have vanished from town," Jacob said, the urgency he'd been feeling reeling out of control. The sleet bounced on his shoulders, stung his face. "We think your husband has them stashed someplace out here."

"Oh, my God." Her face paled, but she didn't waste time asking more questions. "Of course," she replied, her voice shaky. "Do whatever you need to do."

Tom motioned three of the men toward the barn, two more men into the house and indicated that the others follow him and Jacob into the pasture.

Even though there was no way the missing women were hidden in the house, they were hoping to find something that might be used as evidence or a clue as to the women's whereabouts.

It took the men only minutes to spread out and begin to walk the property. As the sleet continued to fall and Jacob looked ahead to the empty pasture, the sick reality of failure ripped through him.

What if he was wrong? What if it wasn't Larry and while they were here wasting their time The Professional was having his party with the women at another location?

As far as his eyes could see there was no structure that could house the women, nothing at all to break up the empty landscape. Where were they? Where could he have stashed them?

It didn't take long for the ground to become more overgrown with tall dead brush and groves of trees, and with each step he took Jacob's last vestiges of hope began to wane.

It had been at least an hour and a half since Layla had been taken, too long to hope that she might still be alive. The darkness of night wasn't far away, adding to Jacob's sense of urgency and his utter despair.

The sleet once again turned to snow as Tom motioned for the others to join him. The five of them came together and Jacob saw that the hopelessness he felt inside himself was mirrored in his brother's dark eyes.

"I'm calling for more men," he said. "There's no way the five of us can cover all this property efficiently."

It would take more precious time for anyone else to arrive on scene, Jacob thought. Too late. They were going to be too late.

"I'm going to press on," he said and motioned toward a rise in the distance. "Maybe from there I can get an eagle-eye view of the rest of the property."

Tom nodded. "I'll go with you." He instructed the others to fan out once again and then fell into step next to Jacob.

The rise in the land was steeper than it had initially appeared and once they crested the top Jacob's heart nearly stopped. Below them, nestled in another grove of trees were two wooden sheds, one small and one large—large enough to hide kidnapped women.

Both buildings were weathered and looked like a hundred other structures that had been built years ago and then left abandoned by the construction of newer buildings.

Adrenaline spiked through him as Tom grabbed his arm. It was obvious his brother thought the same thing that Jacob did, that they'd found Larry's lair.

"We can't just rush in," Tom said with renewed urgency in his voice. "You go to the left and I'll go to the right. We need to take a look inside and assess things before we just barge in."

Jacob nodded, his gaze narrowed as he surveyed the geography. Although there appeared to be nobody around, the last thing he wanted was to be seen approaching the building. Right now the element of surprise was on their side and he wanted to keep it that way.

His heart thrummed a rapid pace as he drew his gun and split up with Tom. Was this it? Was this the place where Larry had planned his party?

When they got inside would they find the same kind of carnage he'd found in the warehouse in Kansas City? His entire being rebelled at the very thought.

The closer he moved to the building the faster his

heart beat. The snow had picked up in pace, lessening visibility and in this case working to their advantage.

This felt right. The location was isolated and if the women were capable of screaming there was nobody around to hear them. It provided easy access for Larry and probably had a way into this area without going past the main house.

By the time he reached the building itself all he could hear was the pounding of his heart in the unnatural silence that snow always brought.

He was glad to see that this side held a side door and that some of the wood had decayed, leaving cracks that would allow him to peer inside.

Before he could look, a scream ripped through the silence, followed by a deep male laugh that Jacob recognized. His blood ran cold and he knew he couldn't wait to assess the situation. The party was happening now and it had to be stopped.

Using his shoulder, he burst through the door and into the shed, his gun in front of him. Everything happened in a split second.

Amazement filled him as he saw the five jail cells constructed inside. Bright red balloons danced around the ceiling, a macabre touch to a scene of horror.

Relief flooded him that all the women were still alive, and a new horror filled him as he saw Larry in the cell with what appeared to be a doped-up Layla.

Before Jacob could act, Larry yanked Layla up before him and held a knife at her throat. "Drop your gun,

Agent Grayson. Dro   eyes."

Layla's eyes were clos   weight in his arms, but the   her whether she was consci

He was vaguely aware of   another woman crying, but his   Larry and the woman he held in

"Let her go. It's over," Jacob s   ...at moment Tom entered through the front door of the building. Jacob held up his hand to keep his brother back, not wanting anything that might force Larry's hand. He tightened his grip on his gun.

"I don't think you heard me, Jacob," Larry replied. "I said drop the gun—both of you—or I'll slit her throat."

"It will be the last act you do before you die," Tom exclaimed.

Larry grinned. "But while I'm in hell I'll enjoy the fact that the last thing I saw was the look on Agent Grayson's face when I killed Layla."

Layla's eyes suddenly opened and in that instant Jacob realized she was not only conscious, but alert. Without warning she shot back her elbow, connecting with Larry's side. He grunted and released his hold on her. Layla flew to the ground and Jacob fired.

The bullet caught Larry in the chest and he reeled backward and fell as a sobbing Layla got back to her feet. She flew out of the cage and toward Jacob and he grab her as she threw herself into his

ged her tight as she wept.

rushed to Larry's side and checked his pulse,

n nodded to Jacob, indicating that the man was dead.
He called for more help as Jacob continued to hold Layla.
"It's over," he said to her. "It's finally over for good."

Tom grabbed the keys from Larry and hurried toward
Brittany's cell. "No," she said. "Get the others out
first."

Within minutes the shed was filled with men and
weeping women. There would be much evidence to
gather, statements to get, cleanup to do. But this time
the cleanup was on their terms, not the terms of the man
who had called himself The Professional.

"I knew you'd find us," Layla said as she finally
moved out of his arms. "I knew if I could just play at
being unconscious long enough you'd have the time you
needed to get here."

A sweet admiration filled him as he thought of what
she'd done when she'd surprised him with the elbow and
then had dropped to the ground, giving Jacob a perfect
shot at Larry. "You're amazing," he said to her and
stroked a finger down the side of her beautiful face.

She gave him a tremulous smile. "I'm a survivor from
way back when."

Then Brittany was in front of him and Layla stepped
back so he could hug the sister he'd thought was lost
forever.

His happiness nearly overwhelmed him, until he realized that now it was safe for Layla to return to her normal life, that now it was time to tell her goodbye.

Chapter 13

It was just after dawn when Jacob and Layla left the sheriff's office and headed back to the cabin. The night had been filled with happy reunions, making statements and gathering facts.

Brittany had gone home with Benjamin and Edie, deciding that she wanted to stay in her childhood home for a while before returning to her house in town. Layla knew it would take a while for Brittany to return to the vivacious, fun-loving woman she'd been before becoming a victim of Larry Norwood.

The other women had been reunited with family and friends and had gone home to heal from the trauma they had endured and the weeks of time that he had stolen from them.

"I feel so bad for Larry's wife and kids," Layla said as she gazed out the passenger window of Jacob's truck. The snow had stopped once again, although it promised to be a cold, blustery day.

"She'll be okay. Apparently she's planning on moving to Chicago where her parents live," Jacob replied. "She had no clue what was going on. She said Larry was always a private man who spent a lot of time out of the house."

"Sounds like their marriage wasn't a good one." She glanced over at him. He'd been unusually quiet on the ride and Layla figured he probably couldn't wait to get rid of her.

"It won't take me long to pack up my things and then if you could just drop me by my house I'd appreciate it."

"No problem."

A wave of depression settled over her. She wasn't sure what she'd wanted him to say, but that wasn't it. There had been a small part of her that had hoped he'd tell her he didn't want to take her home, tell her that he wanted to keep her with him forever.

But, you've never been a forever kind of girl, she reminded herself, and Jacob wasn't a forever kind of man. It was time for her to get back to her sad, lonely life and pretend that it was exactly as she'd planned it, exactly what she wanted.

When they reached the cabin her heart squeezed tight in her chest once again. This was where she'd fallen in love for the very first time. It had only taken days, but she felt as close to Jacob as if they'd been together for months. It felt as if all the other relationships she'd had in the past were just practice for the real thing with him.

Tell him how you feel, a little voice whispered inside her as they entered the living room. But she knew she wasn't going to do that. What was the point? It was better to just walk away than to put her heart on the line and let him reject her. She'd been able to handle other rejections, but his would destroy her.

As she walked into the bedroom to gather her things, he threw himself on the recliner. Whether he knew it or not, he was a much different man than he'd been when she'd first arrived.

She knew he'd always be haunted by the women they hadn't been able to save, but his nemesis was dead, his sister had been found and Jacob had reawakened to life in the days Layla had been with him.

She told herself it was enough for her, that she was content knowing he'd get on with his life and be in a better place than when she'd first arrived here. But as she began to pack her clothes back in the suitcase hot tears burned at her eyes.

Was it so wrong to want to be a forever kind of woman? Was it so wrong to love Jacob enough to want to spend her life with him? They'd been through so much together. They belonged together, but her wishing it didn't make it so.

By the time she had her suitcase packed she had her

emotions back under control. As she reentered the living room Jacob got out of his chair to take the suitcase from her.

"All set?" he asked, his eyes shuttered and showing no emotion.

She nodded. "Back to real life." She forced a cheerfulness into her voice. "At least I'll be home for Christmas." She glanced at the silly little tree they'd decorated with aluminum stars and emotion once again threatened to consume her.

As he carried the suitcase out the front door Layla took one last look around the cabin, remembering laughing with him as they'd talked about Christmases past and decorated their little tree, comforting him as he'd sat in the chair after telling them about The Professional and making love with him beneath the homemade quilt in the bedroom.

There was no question she'd carry a piece of him with her for the rest of her life. He had imprinted into her heart in a way nobody else had ever managed to do.

Leaving the cabin, she hurried to the truck where Jacob was waiting to take her back to her life. "What are your plans now?" she asked when they were headed into town.

"Spend some time with Brittany and the rest of my family, help Tom finish up the last of the details with the case and beyond that I'm not sure. Why?" He didn't look at her but rather kept his gaze focused on the road.

"I was just curious," she replied with forced lightness.

"You know, if you're ever in the market to buy a house I know the best Realtor in town."

He gave her a faint smile. "Yeah, so do I."

The closer they got to her house the tighter emotion pressed thick in her chest. Saying goodbye was never easy, but telling Jacob goodbye seemed like the most difficult thing she'd ever done in her life.

Sure, they would see each other around town, maybe bump into one another on the streets and each time they did she knew she'd feel the ache of his absence deep within her.

"It's going to be a special Christmas for all of you with Brittany finally home," she said. How she wished she were going to be a part of their celebration.

"Yeah, it's definitely going to be a Christmas to remember." His voice wasn't cool, but she felt the distance radiating from him. It was as if he'd already moved on without her and had no desire to look back.

By the time they reached her house she'd fallen silent, had no more words to give him. Her heart weighed a million pounds as they walked up to her front door and he set the suitcase down on the porch.

"Thanks doesn't seem enough for what you did for me," she said.

For a moment she saw something soft in his eyes. "I didn't do for you anymore than you did for me." That softness fled as if it had never really been there. "I'd say we're even."

Even. The word resonated in her soul. She didn't want

to be even. She wanted him to need her, to want her for the rest of their lives. *Even* felt cold and impersonal.

"Be happy, Jacob," she said with her love for him nearly choking her throat.

"You do the same." Before anything else could be said he turned on his heels and walked back to his truck. She watched from the front porch as he drove off without a backward glance.

As she unlocked her door she fought back the tears that threatened to fall. *Silly to be so upset,* she thought as she dragged her suitcase over the threshold and into the entryway.

She was used to men walking away from her, but what made Jacob different was that this time her heart had been completely involved. This time she'd been desperately, hopelessly in love.

Dragging her suitcase into the bedroom, she tried to focus on all the things she needed to do to get back to her normal life. First on her list was to retrieve Mr. Whiskers from the vet's office. Second on her list was to try to figure out a way how to stop loving Jacob Grayson.

At this thought she sat on the edge of her bed and let the tears that she'd desperately been trying to hold back fall.

"So, now that you've rejoined the living when are you going to get out of this place?" Caleb asked Jacob. He and Portia had stopped by the cabin for a visit and Jacob was more than happy for the unexpected company.

It had been a week since Larry Norwood had been killed and all the women had been rescued, seven full days since he'd taken Layla home.

"I don't know, I'm thinking maybe I'll stay here through the winter and then look for something to buy in town in the spring." Jacob frowned thoughtfully. "I'm still not sure I'm ready to rejoin all of humanity."

"What are you brooding about now?" Portia asked.

"I'm not brooding," he protested.

"Yes, you are," she countered. "You've been moody and brooding for the last week. I would think you'd be on top of the world with that creep dead and all the women safe and sound."

"I am on top of the world," Jacob replied, his frown deepening as Portia gave him a disbelieving look. "I'm fine," he assured her, but the truth of the matter was he wasn't fine.

He'd always been a man alone, but he'd never been a lonely man until now, without Layla. She'd breezed into the cabin and had not only brought life back to him, but had also brought love.

He missed the sound of her voice and the clack of her high heels on the floor. He ached for the softness in her eyes and her breathy little sighs as he'd made love to her.

Since she'd been gone he felt as if he'd lost his very best friend, the person who stirred not only his passion but made him laugh and made him want to share all the pieces of himself.

He'd thought she cared about him. There had been moments when she'd gazed at him with such a lightness in her eyes, when she'd touched him with such sweet tenderness that he thought he felt her love for him. And yet she'd walked away without a word, letting him know he was not important in her life.

"You've heard that we're doing a big Christmas gathering at Benjamin and Edie's on Christmas Eve," Caleb said, pulling Jacob from his thoughts of love lost.

"Yeah, Tom mentioned it to me."

"According to Edie, Walt and Margaret are already fighting over who is going to cook what for the meal," Portia said.

Edie's grandfather Walt had briefly moved in with Benjamin and had battled with Margaret, the woman who had been the housekeeper, over the cooking. Somehow in the midst of those initial battles love had blossomed between the two senior citizens and Margaret had moved with Walt to his house in town.

"What do you want Santa to bring you, Jacob?" Portia asked.

"Layla." The name left his lips and he stared at Portia in horror. He'd only meant to think it. He hadn't meant to say it out loud.

"Ah, so that's how it is," Caleb exclaimed with a grin. "I thought I sensed something going on between the two of you."

Jacob stared at his brother and then looked at Portia.

"I'm in love with her," he confessed and he knew his heartache was evident in those five words.

Portia sat back on the sofa and held Jacob's gaze. "That's interesting because she's in love with you."

"Yeah, right," Jacob replied drily. "Trust me, she made it clear to me from the very beginning that she didn't care about relationships."

"But that's not true," Portia replied. She leaned forward. "Jacob, I've known Layla since we were both in grade school. I've never known a woman who needs to be loved more than her, but for years her father told her that she wasn't worthy of love, that she was worthless and no man would ever want her."

Jacob's stomach twisted as he thought of Layla as a vulnerable child dealing with the abuse of her father.

"I've tried to explain to her that love is a verb, that when you're in love you have to do things to show it and you have to talk about it, but she has her defenses so high she doesn't understand." Portia grabbed Caleb's hand. "She's used to men walking away from her, and they walk away because she doesn't give them a reason to stay, she never tells anyone what she wants. But she told me how much she loves you and she's been sick since you two parted ways."

Was it possible what Portia said was true? A tiny ray of hope flared in his heart. Was it possible that both of them had been so afraid of being hurt again they'd let the best thing that could happen walk out of their lives?

"You know, when we Grayson men finally figure out what we want, we usually go after it," Caleb said.

What if Portia was wrong? What if he went to her and spilled his guts and she laughed at him? What if he put his heart on the line with her and she turned him down?

It couldn't hurt any more than it did now. Suddenly what he wanted to do more than anything was let her know that she was worthy, that he loved her with a depth that would last through eternity.

He got out of his chair, driven by the same kind of urgency that had driven him when he'd been hunting for her when she'd been kidnapped. He felt that if he didn't tell her how he felt right now, if he didn't take a chance with her in the next few minutes, he'd explode.

"She's probably at her office," Portia said as he pulled on his coat. She and Caleb got off the sofa and Portia grabbed Jacob by the arms. "If this isn't for forever, if you don't love her with every fiber of your being, then don't bother with her and just leave her alone."

"I can't imagine living without her." His voice was husky with emotion.

Portia nodded and smiled. "Then go get your woman, Jacob."

Minutes later as Jacob drove toward town, doubts began to assail him. What if Portia didn't know what was truly in Layla's heart?

For all he knew in the last week Layla had started dating somebody else in town. He thought of a stop he needed to make before he saw Layla…if he decided to see Layla.

Maybe he was just one of those fools who were forever destined to fall in love with women who didn't have the capacity to love them back.

He eased his foot up on the gas pedal, suddenly unsure what he was going to do.

Layla stared out her office window and tried to fight against the depression that had been a constant companion for the last week.

There was nothing worse than being depressed at Christmastime. The night after she'd gotten home she'd spent the evening decorating her house for the holiday, but all the tinsel and bright lights couldn't pierce through the hollow ache that had invaded her chest. Nothing in her life had prepared her for this kind of heartbreak.

She should just go home. Nobody was going to buy or sell a home so close to the holiday. She was just wasting time sitting here when she could be home with Mr. Whiskers.

Deciding to do just that, she grabbed her purse from the floor and set it on her desk, and it was at that moment she saw him approaching from across the street, a bright red box tucked beneath one arm.

Jacob. Even as she stared at him, she told herself she didn't want to see him, wasn't ready to face him yet. Still, her eyes drank in the sight of him.

At some point since she'd last seen him he'd gotten

a haircut and he walked with a new sense of pride, of confidence that only increased his attractiveness.

As he saw her through the window he smiled and she wanted to weep. She steeled herself as he opened the door and came in, bringing with him the scent of the cold air and a faint whisper of his cologne.

"Well, look what the wind blew in," she said as she stood and forced the lightness into her voice that had always served her well. "If it isn't the town's latest hero and the newest member of law enforcement."

"So you've heard that I'm going to be a deputy," he said, stopping just short of her desk.

"The whole town has heard and has applauded the move by Tom to hire you. You couldn't come with better credentials than being an ex-FBI agent and the man who brought down The Professional."

She wanted to touch him, to run her fingers over the curve of his lips, to press herself against him and feel safe and loved for one last time.

Instead she sat back in her chair to give herself as much distance from him as possible. "So, what are you doing here?"

"I brought you something." He set the red package on the desk in front of her.

She stared at it and then back at him. "Why?"

He jammed his hands into his pockets and shrugged. "Because I felt like it. Go on, open it."

What was he doing? Why was he torturing her? Her

fingers trembled as she unwrapped the paper to reveal a shoe box. She looked up at him again in confusion.

"I couldn't find shoes like the ones you kicked off the day Norwood grabbed you, the ones that were ruined by the snow," he said.

She opened the box and pulled back the inside paper to reveal a pair of bright red sling-back pumps with tiny white bows. They were the most beautiful shoes she'd ever seen.

Tears blurred her vision and suddenly she was mad, mad that he thought she'd want a pair of shoes when all she really wanted was him.

"You crazy fool," she exclaimed. "I don't care about shoes. All I really care about is you." She stared up at him, appalled by her outburst.

His eyes narrowed and he pulled his hands from his pockets. "Do you mean that?"

Tension filled the air, a tension of expectancy that pressed tight against Layla's chest. Did she tell him the truth or did she make a joke out of it? Before she could decide he walked around the desk and pulled her to her feet.

"I just had a talk with Portia," he said. "She reminded me that love is a verb and that it's something you do as well as something you feel. I feel it, Layla, and I decided it was time I act on it."

Her heart began to beat faster but fear kept her frozen in place. "Is this some kind of a joke?" she finally asked.

"Does this feel like a joke?" He pulled her into his arms and took her lips with his in a kiss that sang of hot, sweet desire.

She pulled away from him as tears stung her eyes. "It doesn't feel like a joke. It feels like passion, but I know how that works and eventually that will be gone and there will be nothing left. I don't want you for a little while. I can't stand the thought of you being just another man who leaves me when the passion is gone."

"Oh, Layla." He reached out and embraced her close again. "There's no question that I feel passion for you. But I also want to be the man who holds you when you cry. I want to listen to everything you have to say, even if it sometimes makes my eyes cross. I love you, Layla, but more importantly I need you. I know what your father did to you, how he told you for years that you didn't matter, and I want to spend every day of the rest of my life showing you how important you are to me."

He stroked a hand through her hair and smiled and in that smile she saw his heart, and she knew that it was hers for the taking.

"I do talk too much," she admitted.

"A charming trait."

"And I don't do mornings very well."

"I can give you plenty of space in the mornings," he replied.

"You'd have to like my cat."

He grinned. "I love Mr. Whiskers and I haven't even met him yet."

"I love you, Jacob." Once again tears burned at her eyes, but this time they were happy tears. "And I want you in my life forever. I love everything about you. You're the man I've waited my entire life to find, and contrary to what my father thought, I am worthy of love. I am worthy of your love."

"Layla, you talk too much," he said as he lowered his lips to hers once again.

This time as his mouth plied hers with heat, she tasted not just his passion, but also the kind of love she'd only dreamed about, the kind that would last for the rest of her life.

Epilogue

The noise in the Grayson house was just shy of deafening. Caleb and Benjamin were in a good-natured argument about football. Peyton's daughter, Lilly, was laughing as Tom tickled her tummy and Edie and Benjamin were refereeing Walt and Margaret as they argued about whose dessert was best, Walt's apple pie or Margaret's pumpkin.

Layla sat in a chair next to the grand Christmas tree and breathed in the sense of family that surrounded her. It was magical, as everything had felt since Jacob had come to her office and proclaimed his love for her.

He'd moved from the cabin into her house that day and for the first time in her life Layla felt as if she was where she belonged, that he was where he belonged.

She now smiled as he came into the living room. He'd left a few minutes before to have a chat with Brittany. "How is she?" she asked as she stood.

He wrapped an arm around her shoulders as they stood before the glittery tree. "She's still pretty fragile."

"It hasn't been that long. She just needs time to heal from the ordeal," Layla replied.

"I don't think she's coming back to her job as a deputy."

Layla leaned into him, loving the way she fit so neatly against him. "Did she mention what her plans are?"

"She wants to stay here with Benjamin and Edie for a while longer and she doesn't know for sure what she wants to do after that."

"She'll be okay, Jacob. She's tough and she's a survivor. You all just need to give her some time and space for her to figure it all out."

"I know," he agreed, then laughed as Lilly released a new giggling scream of delight. "Just think, next year there will be another little one with Portia's baby here."

"If we work really hard we could make it two new babies here by next Christmas," she replied.

His eyes burned with a new intensity as he pulled her even closer to him. "I'd like that."

She grinned at him. "You just like the working on it."

"That, too," he agreed with his sexy grin. He sobered and released the sigh of a contented man. "It doesn't get any better than this—family all together, the scent of great food in the air and the woman I love more than life itself standing in my arms."

As he kissed her he warmed her from the very top of her head down to her toes that were encased in the red high heels he'd bought for her.

She returned his kiss and realized all she'd really needed to find happiness was Jacob Grayson and the belief that she was worth every good thing that came her way.

He broke the kiss and held her gaze. "I promise you, Layla, I'm going to love you for the rest of my life."

She gazed up at him with wide eyes. "But you never make promises."

"I only make ones that I intend to keep," he replied. "Now, let's go eat some of that apple and pumpkin pie and then get home so we can work on giving Lilly a new little cousin."

She thrilled not just with the promise his lips had made, but also with the promise that warmed his eyes, the sweet promise of enduring love.

* * * * *

COMING NEXT MONTH

Available March 29, 2011

#1651 ALWAYS A HERO
Justine Davis

#1652 SECRET AGENT SHEIK
Desert Sons
Linda Conrad

#1653 SPECIAL OPS AFFAIR
All McQueen's Men
Jennifer Morey

#1654 STRANDED WITH HER EX
Jill Sorenson

ROMANTIC SUSPENSE

SRSCNM0311

REQUEST YOUR FREE BOOKS!

2 FREE NOVELS
PLUS
2 FREE GIFTS!

ROMANTIC SUSPENSE

Sparked by Danger, Fueled by Passion.

YES! Please send me 2 FREE Silhouette® Romantic Suspense novels and my 2 FREE gifts (gifts are worth about $10). After receiving them, if I don't wish to receive any more books, I can return the shipping statement marked "cancel." If I don't cancel, I will receive 4 brand-new novels every month and be billed just $4.24 per book in the U.S. or $4.99 per book in Canada. That's a saving of at least 15% off the cover price! It's quite a bargain! Shipping and handling is just 50¢ per book in the U.S. and 75¢ per book in Canada.* I understand that accepting the 2 free books and gifts places me under no obligation to buy anything. I can always return a shipment and cancel at any time. Even if I never buy another book, the two free books and gifts are mine to keep forever.

240/340 SDN FC95

Name	(PLEASE PRINT)	
Address		Apt. #
City	State/Prov.	Zip/Postal Code

Signature (if under 18, a parent or guardian must sign)

Mail to the **Reader Service:**
IN U.S.A.: P.O. Box 1867, Buffalo, NY 14240-1867
IN CANADA: P.O. Box 609, Fort Erie, Ontario L2A 5X3

Not valid for current subscribers to Silhouette Romantic Suspense books.

Want to try two free books from another line?
Call 1-800-873-8635 or visit www.ReaderService.com.

* Terms and prices subject to change without notice. Prices do not include applicable taxes. Sales tax applicable in N.Y. Canadian residents will be charged applicable taxes. Offer not valid in Quebec. This offer is limited to one order per household. All orders subject to credit approval. Credit or debit balances in a customer's account(s) may be offset by any other outstanding balance owed by or to the customer. Please allow 4 to 6 weeks for delivery. Offer available while quantities last.

Your Privacy—The Reader Service is committed to protecting your privacy. Our Privacy Policy is available online at www.ReaderService.com or upon request from the Reader Service.

We make a portion of our mailing list available to reputable third parties that offer products we believe may interest you. If you prefer that we not exchange your name with third parties, or if you wish to clarify or modify your communication preferences, please visit us at www.ReaderService.com/consumerschoice or write to us at Reader Service Preference Service, P.O. Box 9062, Buffalo, NY 14269. Include your complete name and address.

SRS11

SAME GREAT STORIES
AND AUTHORS!

Starting April 2011,
Silhouette Romantic Suspense will
become Harlequin Romantic Suspense,
but rest assured that this series will
continue to be the ultimate destination
for sweeping romance and heart-racing
suspense with the same great authors
you've come to know and love!

*Selene wanted nothing to do with the father of her son,
Alex; but Aristedes had other plans...that included them.*

*Read on for an sneak peek from
THE SARANTOS SECRET BABY by Olivia Gates,
available April 2011, only from Harlequin Desire.*

"You were right to turn my marriage offer down," Aristedes said.

And Selene found her voice at last, found the words that would not betray the blow he'd dealt her. "Thanks for letting me know. You didn't have to come all the way here, though. You could have just let it go. I left yesterday with the understanding that this case is closed."

Before the hot needles behind her eyes could dissolve into an unforgivable display of stupidity and weakness, she began to close the door.

The door stopped against an immovable object. His flat palm.

"I can't accept that." His voice was low, leashed.

What did her tormentor mean now? Was he ending one game only to start another?

She raised eyes as bruised as her self-respect to his, found nothing there but solemnity and determination.

Before she could voice her confusion, he elaborated. "I never let anything go unless I'm certain it's unworkable. I realize I made you an unworkable offer, and that's why I'm withdrawing it. I'm here to offer something else. A workability study."

She leaned against the door, thankful for its support and partial shield. "Your son and I are not a business venture you can test for feasibility."

His gaze grew deeper, made her feel as if he was trying to delve into her mind, take control of it. "It's actually the other way around. I'm the one who would be tested."

She shook her head. "Why bother? I know—and *you* know—you're not workable. Not with me."

His spectacular eyebrows lowered over eyes she felt were emitting silver hypnosis. "You're right again. Neither you nor I have any reason to believe that isn't the truth. The only truth. It might be best for both you and Alex to never hear from me again, to forget I exist. But then again, maybe not. I'm only asking for the chance for both of us to find out for certain. You believe I'm unworkable in any personal relationship. I've lived my life based on that belief about myself. I never really had reason to question it. But I have one now. In fact, I have two."

Find out what happens in
THE SARANTOS SECRET BABY *by Olivia Gates,*
available April 2011, only from Harlequin Desire.